"I would have helped." Gabriel said it with a frown when he saw that she stood beyond the buggy, waiting for him.

"I'm not as helpless as you think," she replied.

A look of hurt flickered in his expression. "I know you're not."

He started toward the store entrance. Lucy instantly felt contrite. "Gabriel," she called, and he stopped and turned. "I'm sorry." She hated the tension between them. He only wanted to help her from her buggy. Why make an issue of it? Because Harley had never treated her so well, she realized.

His softened expression told her she was forgiven. He held out his hand to Susie. "Come, little one. Let's see what's inside."

Lucy, following behind them, realized that she was beginning to care a lot for this sensitive man, and she didn't know what she was going to do about it.

Rebecca Kertz was first introduced to the Amish when her husband took a job with an Amish construction crew. She enjoyed watching the Amish foreman's children at play and swapping recipes with his wife. Rebecca resides in Delaware with her husband and dog. She has a strong faith in God and feels blessed to have family nearby. Besides writing, she enjoys reading, doing crafts and visiting Lancaster County.

Books by Rebecca Kertz

Love Inspired

Loving Her Amish Neighbor

Women of Lancaster County

A Secret Amish Love
Her Amish Christmas Sweetheart
Her Forgiving Amish Heart
Her Amish Christmas Gift
His Suitable Amish Wife
Finding Her Amish Love

Lancaster County Weddings

Noah's Sweetheart
Jedidiah's Bride
A Wife for Jacob
Elijah and the Widow
Loving Isaac

Visit the Author Profile page at Harlequin.com for more titles.

Loving Her Amish Neighbor

Rebecca Kertz

LOVE INSPIRED
INSPIRATIONAL ROMANCE

LOVE INSPIRED®

INSPIRATIONAL ROMANCE

Recycling programs
for this product may
not exist in your area.

ISBN-13: 978-1-335-48890-9

Loving Her Amish Neighbor

Copyright © 2021 by Rebecca Kertz

This edition published by arrangement with Harlequin Books S.A.

For questions and comments about the quality of this book, please contact us
at CustomerService@Harlequin.com.

Love Inspired
22 Adelaide St. West, 40th Floor
Toronto, Ontario M5H 4E3, Canada
www.Harlequin.com

Printed in U.S.A.

What time I am afraid, I will trust in thee.
—*Psalms* 56:3

For my husband, Kevin, for his patience,
his kindness and his enduring love.

Chapter One

∼

Late springtime, New Berne,
Lancaster County, Pennsylvania

"You be a *gut* girl for your aunt," Lucy Schwartz said as she lifted her four-year-old daughter into her arms for one last hug, something that was getting more difficult with her advancing pregnancy. "I'll be back to get you after supper."

"Why can't I stay with you?" Susie blinked pretty pale blue eyes up at her, eyes so like her father's—Lucy's late husband.

"I have work to do, *dochter*," she explained, her fingers caressing Susie's cheek. "You'll have more fun with *Endie* Nancy and your cousins."

"Come on, Susie!" her cousin Sarah cried as, *kapp* strings flying, she ran toward their big red barn beyond their dirt driveway.

Susie wriggled to get down. "I'll see you later, *Mam*." Blue skirts flipping enough to show her sneakers, she ran after Nancy's daughter. "Hold up, Sarah! I'm coming! Hold up!"

Lucy grinned as her child scampered off. "My Susie's got energy, that's for sure," she said with a chuckle. She turned to her sister-in-law Nancy. "*Danki* for keeping her."

Nancy smiled, watching as the two girls disappeared inside the barn before meeting Lucy's gaze. "We love having her. You know we're always here to help in any way we can."

Blinking rapidly, Lucy nodded. "I appreciate it." Her marriage to Nancy's brother hadn't been a happy one. Still, her sister-in-law had stepped up to help Lucy after Harley had passed on. Her relationship with Nancy had actually improved since Harley's death.

"I need to go home, collect my baked goods and deliver them."

"If you need us to keep her overnight, let us know," Nancy said as she walked with Lucy toward her buggy.

Lucy nodded. "I will." She heard wild cries of joy as Sarah and Susie ran out of the barn. Sarah had a rope wrapped around her waist while Susie held on to the ends behind her, urging her on. "I guess Sarah is the horse this morning," she said with a chuckle.

Nancy laughed. "No doubt Susie will get her turn this afternoon."

Lucy climbed into her buggy and picked up the leathers. "Is there anything you need from the store?"

"*Nay*, but I appreciate you asking."

With a wave, Lucy left the property and headed home. She'd baked various cakes, cookies and pies yesterday and packaged them for sale this morning. There were enough for King's General Store and Peter's Pockets, a dessert shop that catered to tourists wanting a taste of Amish. It would be the perfect place to feature her bakery items.

As she steered the buggy, she thought about the changes in her life since she'd married Harley Schwartz, a widower. The union had been arranged by her father. At nineteen, she hadn't wanted to marry, but her father had made it clear that she'd be left alone to fend for herself otherwise. And then her heart had melted after seeing Susie, Harley's two-week-old daughter. Susie's mother had died in childbirth, and the tiny babe had no mother to love and care for her. For Susie's sake, Lucy had agreed to wed the baby's father.

As if marriage hadn't been enough of a change, Harley had taken her from her Amish community in Indiana and brought her to live in New Berne, Pennsylvania, where she knew no one. She'd been forced to leave her little brother Seth behind and she'd missed him terribly. She still did.

Eventually she and Harley had settled into a comfortable life. Harley had worked and supported them while Lucy kept house and took care of Susie, whom she adored.

A little over four years later, Harley died in a truck accident at his construction job. While their marriage hadn't been ideal—Lucy had wanted more from it—Harley was a good man, and it was a tragedy for him to die at only twenty-nine years old.

The settlement money from Harley's employer helped her make ends meet, but she knew the money wouldn't last forever. With Harley gone five months now, Lucy had to earn a living to support Susie, her unborn child and herself. After Nancy asked her to bring sweets for Visiting Sunday last weekend, Lucy remem-

bered how much her late husband had loved her cakes
and pies. Her ability to bake had been the one thing
Harley had raved about, and he'd never been one to
give compliments to Lucy, the replacement for his beloved dead wife.

Selling baked goods seemed the best way for her to
earn money and stay at home raising the children. With
that in mind, Lucy had approached several local shops
with samples of her baked sweets to pitch the idea of
selling her wares on consignment. The shop owners
had loved her bakery samples and were happy to do
business with her. Today would be her first delivery
of her sweets.

The day was bright and balmy, which made it a perfect morning for her errands. Lucy smiled as she passed
horses galloping across the paddock of a nearby farm.
The warm breeze caressed her face, bringing with it the
scents of spring blossoms, new grass and farm animals.

As the steady clip-clop of her horse's shoed hooves
hit the pavement, Lucy wondered with a smile if Susie
was enjoying herself. Was she playing hide-and-seek
or tag with her cousins?

A car came up behind her, and Lucy moved onto the
shoulder of the road to allow it to pass. She was just
easing back into the lane when a sudden loud rev of an
engine alerted her to another motor vehicle approaching from behind. She didn't have time to move to the
shoulder again, but instead, held tightly to the reins as
she waited for it to pass. Something clipped the back
of her buggy hard, startling her, and she cried out. Her
mare whinnied and spooked before the animal took off,
Lucy holding on for dear life. Her horse and buggy ca-
reened off the road and bounced along the embankment

as the car zoomed past. Blackie's flight jostled her vehicle. She held on to the leathers as she tried to calm her horse while her right side slammed against the side wall.

Reaching a hand out to brace herself, Lucy bumped her head and felt a jolt along her arm as her buggy jerked and dipped before finally coming to a complete stop in a ditch, tilting to one side. Grabbing the dashboard, she looked up through the windshield. The driver of the black car had sped off, either not caring or not realizing that he'd left the scene of the accident he'd caused.

She took a deep breath, let go of the dash and wrapped the leather reins around her left hand. Her head ached, and pain throbbed down her right side. Lucy cradled her swollen belly with her right hand, gasping with the movement, but the ache in her wrist quickly eased. "We're *oll recht, bubbel*." She felt no twinges along her abdomen. "You and I are going to be fine."

She had to get out of the buggy. She tried to open the door on her side so she could slide out through the opening but there was no room. And if the vehicle toppled over, she and her baby would be crushed.

She needed help but had no way to call anyone. Some Amish in the country had cell phones for work or emergencies, but it was a luxury Harley had told her they couldn't afford.

Her only hope was for someone to drive by, see her predicament and stop to help.

Lucy closed her eyes and sent up a silent prayer to the Lord for assistance.

She finished with an "amen" and pressed her fingertips to the place on her head she'd been injured. She was startled when her hand came away with blood. Her distress intensified as she worked to figure out her next move. She checked her surroundings, moving carefully so as not to shift the buggy. Blackie stood, seemingly unhurt, still attached to her vehicle. At least her buggy was far enough off the road to avoid being hit again. *Thank You, Lord.*

Lucy frowned. Now what was she going to do? She reevaluated her injuries. Except for a slight headache and the few areas on her side that ached, the only other thing she felt was a throbbing pain along her right arm down through her wrist. She didn't think her injuries were serious. As long as her baby was all right…

Heart beating wildly, she breathed deeply to calm herself then sent up a silent prayer of thanks that Susie was safe with Nancy. Until someone happened along, the only thing she could do was wait. She leaned back against the seat with her eyes closed, praying that her injuries were mild and help would come soon.

The clip-clop of horse hooves on the road behind her caught her attention. Lucy opened her eyes. The sound stopped. Had she imagined it? She prayed that she hadn't.

"Hallo?" a man's voice asked from the street side of the carriage.

Relief hit her hard. Someone had stopped to help. She hadn't imagined the sound of another buggy. She sensed his presence before he appeared at the open window.

His gaze sharpened as he looked inside. "Are you *oll recht*?"

"I think so." Lucy met the man's gaze as he assessed her condition, his expression filled with concern. He was Amish with dark hair under his straw hat, brown eyes, and a jagged, raised scar across his left cheek. She tried not to stare, focusing instead on the solid maroon color of his long-sleeved shirt and black suspenders that reached over each shoulder.

"I'm Gabriel Fisher. What's your name?"

"Lucy," she said. "Lucy Schwartz."

"Lucy," he said calmly, "I'm going to help you."

She met his concerned gaze. *"Danki."*

"What hurts?"

"Mostly my head and arm." She touched a hand to the side of her head again and saw more blood on her fingers. "I'm bleeding." She swallowed hard as she let go of the reins to rub her belly with her left hand.

He lowered his gaze to where she cradled her abdomen. "Try not to move," he commanded, but his tone was gentle. "Anything else hurt?"

"My right side."

Gabriel nodded. "I need to get you to a doctor."

"I thought about climbing out, but I was afraid the buggy would move and crush me."

"Ja, it looks unstable but I can fix that. Hold on."

She closed her eyes. Why did she feel so tired? Because of her pregnancy or an injury? Lucy wanted nothing more than to lie down and rest. This past year, with her husband's death and with all that had come afterward, had taken a toll.

She no longer heard Gabriel's voice. Her eyes shot open and she looked to where he'd stood. He was gone. Her throat tightened as she started to panic, and she struggled to breathe evenly. "Gabriel?"

Silence.

"Gabriel!"

"I'm here." His voice sounded muffled, as if he lay under her vehicle. "I'm checking the damage to your buggy." His head popped up again in the window on the street side.

"Blackie? My mare? Is she *oll recht*?"

"Amazingly, *ja*." His smile was soft, reassuring. "I'm going to unhitch her and secure her to my buggy. *Ja?*"

She nodded then grimaced at the movement.

"A simple *ja* would do," he said gently. "You mustn't move or you might injure yourself further."

"I'm fine."

"Let's let the doctor decide that, hmm?"

Releasing the reins, Lucy closed her eyes as she sensed him leave her. She felt her rising panic again when he didn't immediately return. "Gabriel?"

"I'm here." His head popped up on her side. "Took care of Blackie." He frowned as his gaze settled on her forehead. "I was on my way home from the lumber-yard. I'm going to shore up the buggy on this side with a two-by-six I have in the back of my buggy. It should just about be long enough."

Gabriel disappeared from sight. Lucy took a calming breath and shut her eyes. When she could see him, she felt better. She gasped, startled, and opened her eyes to find him leaning inside the buggy, his head close to her. "I'm going to wedge the board between your buggy and the ground," he said softly. "It hasn't rained all week. The dirt should be hard enough to hold the weight." He studied her with a frown. "Lucy, are you with me?"

She met his worried gaze. "*Ja*, I'm here."

He smiled. "Give me a minute. The carriage may shift a bit. Don't panic. *Ja?*"

"I understand."

"*Gut* girl," he praised.

The buggy shifted, and Lucy instinctively grabbed

onto the edge of the seat with both hands. She gasped as pain surged through her right wrist. She fought back tears but held on.

He rose to his feet, peered in at her. "That should hold but it's best if I bring you out the opposite side."

The street side, Lucy thought. The sound of an engine broke the silence. She tensed, locking gazes with Gabriel before he turned to face the approaching vehicle. She detected a harsh, high-pitched sound as if the vehicle was braking hard, and she closed her eyes and prayed. *Please, Lord, save us.* Gabriel was in as much danger as she if her buggy was hit again.

When she opened her eyes, Gabriel was walking away until she could no longer see him. The sound of male voices rumbled in her ears before he returned with an *Englisher.*

"Don't you worry, miss. We'll get you out in a sec." The man was big, gruff and tattooed. He wore a baseball cap with the brim turned backward, a dark T-shirt and jeans. His appearance should have frightened her, but as he smiled at her, she wasn't afraid. "Bert Hadden, miss," he introduced himself as he stood beside Gabriel.

Her attention shifted to Gabriel, who captured her gaze reassuringly. "Gabriel," she whispered.

"I've got you, Lucy," he assured her. "Bert is going to give us some help. He's called someone with a horse trailer to take care of Blackie for us."

"My brother-in-law," Bert explained. "He and I own a farm less than a mile from here." He grinned, displaying stained, uneven teeth, but there was something about him that convinced her he was harmless. "How did this happen?" he asked as Gabriel skirted her vehicle to the other side.

"Blackie got spooked after a car hit the back end of my buggy."

"And the driver didn't stop?"

"*Nay*. He kept going."

"Can you give a description? We need to tell the police."

"She will when she's ready," Gabriel said. "If she remembers what the car looked like." He unlatched the door. "Bert, make sure the buggy is braced well. I've got another two-by-six if we need it."

"Right." Bert grinned at her.

Gabriel slowly climbed into the buggy. The vehicle shifted under his weight, and Lucy inhaled sharply. "Bert?" he called.

"It's fine, Gabe. The board—she's gonna hold." Bert propped his body against the outer wall of the buggy to further brace it.

"Lucy, slide my way if you can," Gabriel urged with one hand extended toward her.

Through every inch she slid her sore body, she fought back tears.

"Stop," he said gently. "Rest easy now. 'Tis *oll recht*. I've got you." He carefully maneuvered closer then paused as if to gauge the seriousness of her injuries. He gave a nod, apparently satisfied that he could move her. "Lucy, lean toward me a little."

She did as he asked. The vehicle rocked a bit. "It's okay," Bert called out. "She's holding steady."

With her gaze focused on Gabriel, Lucy pushed up with her hands to stand, then cried out when a sharp pain in her wrist stopped her. "I'm *oll recht*," she assured him. "Just give me a minute."

"Need help?" Bert asked, his head appearing briefly in the window on Lucy's other side.

"We're fine," Gabriel assured him.

Using only her left hand, Lucy managed to move a few inches closer to Gabriel. She started to rise and nearly fell back onto the seat, but he reached out to steady her.

"I have you." He slipped his arms around then beneath her and lifted her.

"You okay in there?" Bert asked.

"All *gut*. Coming out now." Cradling her against his chest, Gabriel turned and, clearly mindful of her injuries, carried her slowly to the street side of the buggy.

Bert was there as Gabriel was ready to step down with her in his arms. "I can take her."

Gabriel shook his head. "I've got her." She heard his sharp intake of breath and saw him grimace as he stepped down, still carrying her weight. Bert reached out to steady him. With the man's help, Gabriel lowered her to the ground.

"I called 9-1-1," Bert said gruffly.

Flashing lights in the distance with a short burst of a siren drew her attention. The emergency vehicle pulled up and parked in front of Lucy's buggy. Two paramedics got out and ran in their direction with a medical bag. Lucy was unsteady on her feet, and Gabriel held her up with his arm around her. "You should sit," he said worriedly.

She met his gaze. "I'll be *oll recht*."

"I know you will," he whispered in her ear, and his breath against it made her shiver.

"Ma'am, we need to examine you. You need to sit or lie down."

Before she could answer, Gabriel lifted her up into his arms again. "Gabriel!" she gasped. Ignoring her outcry, he carried her to his buggy where he set her in the open doorway.

He stepped back, his expression shuttered. He moved out of the way, and the female EMT took his place.

"Can you tell me what happened?" she asked as she opened her medical bag and pulled out a stethoscope.

"My buggy was hit by a car. I was forced off the road. The driver didn't stop."

The woman nodded as she listened first to her baby bump then to her heart, and finally she placed the listening device to her neck and throat. "Your baby's heartbeat is strong," she said with a smile as she put her medical equipment back in her bag. "You need an ultrasound to be sure he's fine."

Lucy nodded. "All right."

"Where do you hurt?" she asked. "You bumped your head." She examined the injury. "A little cut. Looks like the wound bled, but bleeding's stopped." She checked Lucy's eyes with a small flashlight. "Headache?"

"A little one coming on." Lucy saw the other paramedic talking with her rescuer. "I hit my right side. It hurts but I don't think it's bad. My right arm hurts, but now I think it's my wrist that's injured. I couldn't use it when I tried to push myself up to stand. I had to use my left."

The paramedic grasped her right hand. She gently manipulated her wrist, and Lucy inhaled sharply. "Can you move your fingers?" Lucy did. "Good. Let's check your elbow and shoulder." A moment later she declared, "They look good, as well. You'll need an X-ray, but nothing seems broken. You most likely have a sprained wrist. We'll need to make sure." The woman smiled. "You're lucky, Lucy. I've been on the scene of many buggy accidents, and most have more tragic results."

"I know." She recalled one such terrible accident that had killed a member of her church community back in Indiana, where she'd spent her childhood.

Gabriel bent as if to pick her up again, but she held up her good hand. "I can stand," she assured him. She stared at her buggy. "How bad?"

"Broken axle," he told her quietly. "Body is in good shape, though."

She met his gaze, nodded. "Could have been worse."

Gabriel studied Lucy and the wild beating of his heart subsided a little. When he'd spied the damaged buggy in the ditch, he'd feared the worst. And when he saw she was pregnant, stark terror struck him.

"You'll see a doctor soon," he said reassuringly. He'd worry until he knew for certain that she was all right. She looked at him, her big beautiful blue eyes filled with gratitude, and he shifted uncomfortably.

"An ambulance is on its way," the male paramedic said. "Lucy, you need to go to the emergency room."

As if summoned, flashing lights and the whine of a siren heralded the ambulance's arrival.

"I'd rather go to the clinic down the road. I have a doctor there. She can help me. I promise I'll go to the hospital if she tells me to."

The paramedics exchanged a look.

"We'll take you there by ambulance," the woman insisted. "No arguments."

Lucy nodded. She grabbed on to Gabriel's arm. "Would you go with me?"

"Do you need me to get in touch with your husband?" he asked quietly.

She shook her head, briefly averting her gaze. "I… I'm a widow."

He felt a jolt; he knew what it was to be hurt and alone. "I'm sorry," he said softly. "I'll go if you want me to."

"Danki," she whispered, her blue eyes filling with relief.

"I'll be right back," he said. "Know anyone who can drive my buggy?" After only two months in New Berne, he was familiar with the medical building with doctors' offices and an urgent care facility. He'd become a patient of a neurologist and a burn specialist because of severe injuries he'd suffered during a house fire.

"I'll do it. I know horses," Bert told him. "Drive lots of wagons. I'll be happy to drive it home for you." He smiled. "I'll call my nephew. He can bring me back for my pickup. And I'll arrange for my brother-in-law to bring your horse home in his trailer. What's the address?"

Gabriel looked at Lucy, who gave Bert her address. He was surprised that she lived about a half mile down the road from him.

"I don't know how to thank you, Bert," Lucy said.

The gruff *Englisher* smiled. "You just did." He shot Gabriel a glance. "You take care of her, and I'll take care of everything else."

The ambulance driver parked and the female EMT swung open the double rear doors. Two ambulance workers pulled out a stretcher and carried it in Lucy's direction.

"Are you sure you want me to go with you?" Gabriel asked.

She nodded. "*Please.* I don't know what I would have done if you hadn't stopped to help me."

The two paramedics helped to lower Lucy onto the stretcher. "Gabriel stays with me," Lucy told him.

It looked as if one of the ambulance workers would object, but then the female medic said, "He can go." The attendants lifted Lucy into the back of the vehicle. They climbed in after her and waited for Gabriel to get in before closing the doors.

When he woke up this morning, Gabriel never thought he'd end up rescuing a woman he'd never met and staying with her while she went to the doctor.

For the first time in a long time, he felt almost… normal. Lucy hadn't been repulsed by his visible burn scar, and it made him feel good.

Chapter Two

Lucy sensed Gabriel's concern before she met his gaze. He sat so closely beside her in the ambulance that his knees brushed the stretcher the paramedics had insisted they transport her on. "I'm sorry," she murmured.

His brow furrowed as he frowned. "Why?"

Without looking at him, she rubbed along the edge of her hairline with light fingertips. Why had she asked a stranger to come with her to the doctor? She stretched her neck slightly to alleviate the stiffness. Her head didn't hurt as much as it had earlier but it ached between her shoulders. "I shouldn't have asked you to come. Maybe you need to get home."

Was he married? She'd feel bad if he was. But if he were married, wouldn't he have gone home? Closing her eyes, Lucy lay still and took several calming breaths before she opened them again.

"I don't," he said with a lopsided sad smile that tugged at her heartstrings. "I don't need to go home."

Lucy felt emotional and afraid. She was pregnant and an accident victim with a young daughter and no husband to take care of her if she was badly hurt. And now she was relying on a stranger's kindness. "Gabriel," she whispered.

"What is it?" he said, looking concerned. "What's wrong?"

She watched the scenery fly by, thankful the driver at least hadn't put on the siren. "My daughter, Susie, is at my sister-in-law Nancy's *haus*. I was supposed to get her after supper. If I can't make it, will you let Nancy know? She'll take care of Susie if I end up in the hospital." Lucy was worried. What was she going to do about the delivery of her cakes and pies? She didn't want all of that baking to go to waste.

"*Ja*, I'll make sure she knows." His expression softened slightly. "Bert has arranged for your buggy to be moved to a carriage shop. He promised to get in touch with an estimate for repairs." He leaned closer and settled a comforting hand on her shoulder. "Don't worry about your *dochter*. If you give me your sister-in-law's address, I'll take a ride over there to tell her."

"I need to take your vitals," the paramedic said before Lucy could answer.

Straightening, Gabriel withdrew his hand, and Lucy felt the loss as the attendant wrapped a blood pressure cuff around her left arm.

After he took a reading, the man checked her pulse. "Blood pressure and pulse are fine." He shined a tiny flashlight in one eye and then the other. "Pupils are normal and reactive. All good signs."

Reassured, Lucy nodded. *"Danki."* Her gaze capturing Gabriel's, she saw that he looked relieved. She closed her eyes and settled her good hand on her belly, hoping, praying that her unborn *bubbel* hadn't been affected by the accident. The paramedic strapped a splint onto her right arm to stabilize it.

She felt the stretcher shift as the vehicle slowed then turned.

"We're here," Gabriel said softly.

The ambulance stopped and the rear doors opened. Gabriel climbed out first. She heard the attendant talking with the paramedics who had treated her at the scene. The rolling stretcher was lowered down by the driver and the man who'd ridden in the back with them.

The female paramedic appeared in her vision as she leaned over Lucy to make eye contact. "We'll come inside with you to give them our report." She accepted a clipboard from the man who'd been in the back with them.

As she was wheeled inside, Lucy sent up a silent prayer of thanks for Gabriel and Bert.

Her eyes flew open. "Gabriel, your buggy—"

"Not to worry. I'll call for a car when you're done."

Lucy sighed with relief. For the first time in a long time, she didn't feel alone.

As they entered the clinic, Lucy lost sight of Gabriel. Her chest tightened and she could hear her own heartbeat as she started to panic. Then she caught a glimpse of a wide-brimmed, banded straw hat. With the realization that he'd followed her stretcher, she felt herself begin to calm again. She'd never met Gabriel before today, yet it felt as if she somehow knew him.

Her stretcher stopped moving, and Lucy waited while the paramedics spoke with the receptionist at the front desk. She heard the words "accident" and "hit and run." Gabriel moved closer to her side, leaning over her, and flashed her a reassuring smile. "How are you feeling?" he asked huskily.

"I'm…" Without thinking, she shifted on the stretcher, then winced and clutched her right hand as pain radiated down her arm to her hand beneath the splint.

"Lucy—" He looked at her with alarm, his dark eyes filling with concern.

She breathed through the pain until it subsided. "I'll be fine."

His expression softened. "They'll be taking you in the back in a few minutes."

He glanced toward the front desk and Lucy studied his arresting features.

Her stretcher began to move as an attendant rolled her toward an open doorway. Lucy rose slightly, needing to see Gabriel before she disappeared into a back room. Her panic started to rise again, making it difficult for her to breathe.

"Wait," she heard Gabriel say. Her stretcher stopped moving. Suddenly, she could see him again as he leaned over her, his features warm and filled with emotion. "I'll wait for you here."

"*Danki*, Gabriel." Her eyes felt scratchy.

Fear kept her silent as she was pushed into a small green room. The ambulance attendants transferred her from the stretcher onto an exam table then left her alone. As she took stock of the room, Lucy prayed for the good health of her baby and for the strength she'd need to face the uncertainty of the days ahead.

She closed her eyes, picturing Gabriel's face, his warm brown eyes, his smooth voice telling her she'd be all right. And her fear started to recede. *Gott* would help her, and knowing Gabriel waited for her out front made it easier to focus on the good and not the bad.

The door opened, and Lucy struggled to sit up as two women entered the room.

"Stay still." The soft command came from a pleasant-looking woman dressed in a white lab coat worn over a floor-length floral dress. "Hello, Lucy," she said. "I am Dr. Benjai, and this is Karen. We're going to take a look at you and see how you're doing." While Karen hovered close by, the doctor gently brushed back her hair to check her injured forehead. "I heard you were in an accident. I see you bumped your head and hurt your arm. Tell me what happened."

Gabriel fidgeted in his seat while he waited for what seemed like forever. Was Lucy all right? He abandoned his chair to pace, his anxiety increasing with each step he took. His left leg burned with every movement, but he didn't care. He was more worried that he had injured her further when he'd lifted her from her buggy.

As he reached one end of the room and turned back, he sensed that others inside the waiting room were staring at him, but he didn't care. He resisted the urge to tug down his hat brim in an attempt to hide his face.

He heard the swish of the glass automatic entry doors opening and looked up. Bert had entered the care center, his gaze searching the room. When he saw him, he headed in Gabriel's direction. "Drove your buggy home." He shoved his hair from his forehead, briefly calling attention to his tattooed hand. "Fred tied up the mare by the barn. Made sure she had water before he left."

"Appreciate it," Gabriel said gratefully. "What can I do to repay you?"

Bert looked horrified by the notion. "Nothing, Gabe," he replied, his voice gruff. "Just glad to help." He nodded toward the reception desk. "How is she doing?"

"I haven't heard yet. She said her right side and arm hurt, but otherwise she feels fine."

Bert nodded. "Good thing she's getting checked out, being pregnant and all." He peered through the glass doors, his hand shielding his face from the sunlight. He was grinning as he faced Gabriel. "I called a friend of mine in the towing business. We were able to push the buggy onto his flatbed. It wasn't easy, 'cause there's something wrong with the axle. Told him to bring her to Lapp's place in Happiness." He paused. "You got a cell phone?"

"Nay." He'd been meaning to get one for business reasons. He made toys and wooden crafts to sell on consignment in area shops. Cell phones were never allowed in his former church district in Ohio, but he hadn't been planning to start up a business then so it hadn't mattered. Here it was permitted, but only for work, never personal reasons. And for emergencies. Lucy needed one, too, he thought. She didn't know him, but still he'd have to convince her to get one, especially being pregnant.

"He'll call with an estimate. I'll stop by and let you know what he says." The big man grinned. "I know where you live now."

Surprise made his face flush. Bert thought that he and Lucy were related. He didn't bother to correct him, although he knew he should. It would be too awkward to confess the truth that Lucy and he were strangers after the way he'd stayed by her side.

Something hit him square in the chest. *Because I'm worried about her*, he told himself. He barely knew her, but now he knew she was his neighbor. He'd moved to New Berne two months ago, but except for arranging consignments and delivering his work to stores, he'd kept mainly to himself.

Gabriel was grateful that the large, kind man covered in tattoos had cared for their horses and vehicles. "If there is anything I can do for you…"

Bert waved his hand in dismissal. "Na. I'm good. It was nice meeting you, Gabe. You and Lucy." His hazel eyes held regret. "Wish it'd been under better circumstances."

"Me, too, Bert. I don't know what we would have done without you."

The man actually blushed. "You would have managed."

"Not as well."

Bert nodded as he turned to leave. "You take care of your girl."

"Bert!" Gabriel called after him, ignoring his comment about his relationship with Lucy. "Will you ask Eli Lapp to leave a message for Lucy about her buggy at King's General Store?"

"Will do. I know the place," Bert assured him. He started toward the door then halted. "How're you getting home?"

"I'll call for a car."

Bert handed him a card. "Here's my number. Call me. I'll come back with my car instead of my pickup. It won't take long for me to come."

"Thank you." Grateful, Gabriel tucked the card beneath his suspender strap near the waistband of his pants.

Without the distraction of the Good Samaritan, Gabriel started to pace again. Step by step, he went over everything that had happened since he'd come upon the scene of Lucy's accident. He felt warmth in his chest as he recalled Lucy pleading with him with her eyes as she'd asked him to ride in the ambulance with her. He liked that she'd needed him, but that didn't mean anything. He was simply being neighborly. Of course, before today he hadn't known she was his neighbor.

Gabriel felt the familiar pins and needles in his leg that meant he'd overused it. He took a seat and rubbed his thigh, prepared to wait for as long as it took until Lucy was released and he could take her home. It was close to noon. He was a little hungry, and despite what she was enduring, he wondered if she'd want to eat once she was released. He'd left the house after a quick cup of coffee and a muffin to make two early morning deliveries on the other side of New Berne before restocking his supply of wood for his shop at the lumberyard. He'd been on his way home when he'd spied Lucy's buggy off the road. After Bert took them to Lucy's, he'd take his buggy to pick up sandwiches. It would be the neighborly thing to do.

What would he do if she were admitted to the hospital? First, he'd tell her sister-in-law as promised. It was possible her family would step in to take care of everything while she recovered. If not, he could ask his sister to help care for Lucy's child.

His leg prickled, making him tense up. He took several deep, calming breaths to relax. The pain would get better. It had to. Lucy would be released soon, then he'd ride home with her so she could rest before he headed over to tell her sister-in-law. Everything would be all right. It had to be. If Lucy wanted her daughter home, he could get Susie for her. As long as the burn in his leg didn't worsen.

It had been a long time since he'd prayed or been to church service. Not since before the fire that had taken his parents and his three other siblings. There had been complications with his burns and the skin grafting surgery that he'd needed, which had extended his recovery time in the hospital and at the uncle's house where he and his only surviving sister Emily had lived until Gabriel had sold their family's farm property and moved with her to New Berne. Although he'd been here almost two months, he hadn't been able to bring himself to attend church in his new community yet. He hated the stares, the looks of pity or dismay whenever someone new saw him. But he could pray. Surprised by the strength of his desire to pray, Gabriel closed his eyes and sent up a silent prayer to *Gott* that Lucy was all right.

Just as he was opening his eyes, a door opened, revealing the back area where she had been taken over an hour ago. Lucy came out, walking gingerly on her own with an Ace bandage around her right wrist to her forearm and carrying a small medicine bottle. The cut on her forehead was barely visible.

Relieved, Gabriel got up and approached her. Her blue eyes brightened when she spotted him. He felt a startling tenderness toward her as her mouth curved up when he reached her. "How did you make out?" he asked.

"*Gut. Danki* for waiting."

"I was worried about you." He settled his gaze briefly on her pregnant belly. "Are you ready to go?" he asked gently.

"*Ja*, I'm done." Grimacing, she held up her bandaged wrist. "The doctor said it's not broken but sprained. It should be fine in a couple of days." She settled a hand against her belly, clearly something she did often during her pregnancy. "I'm in *gut* shape, considering."

Gabriel was relieved. "Thanks be to *Gott*," he murmured. He gestured toward the glass entry doors. "Bert's going to give us a ride. Why don't you sit for a minute while I call him?" When Lucy nodded, he helped her into a chair then hurried to ask the receptionist if he could use the phone.

Bert arrived five minutes after Gabriel's call. "I was across the street, picking up a few groceries."

Gabriel thanked him, and Lucy smiled. "That's kind of you," she said.

The man smiled. "I'm parked up front."

"Are you ready to go?" Gabriel asked her.

"*Ja.*" She pushed herself up, wobbled on her feet.

He steadied her. "Are you sure you're *oll recht*?"

She beamed at him. "I'm fine."

He slipped his arm through hers and led her through the doors to where Bert had parked his car, a silver four-door sedan. Gabriel instinctively reached to open the car door for her. Lucy glanced back to lock gazes with him. He felt the sharp impact of her bright blue eyes and attempted to smile, but she quickly averted her gaze. Leaning forward, he held the door open to let her pass. As she brushed close to him, he became aware of the scent of vanilla and honey intermingled with a light fragrance unique to Lucy.

Gabriel was conscious of the warmth of her skin as he clasped her arm and lowered her carefully inside.

He couldn't help but notice how her eyes glittered in a pale face as he got into the back seat. "It won't take long to get you home and more comfortable."

She nodded and tentatively touched her right side with her left hand but stopped when she saw him looking.

After a short journey, Bert pulled into Lucy's driveway and parked.

"Thanks, Bert," Gabriel said. He handed him some money. "For gas."

Bert brushed it aside. "Nope. I'm good." He glanced toward Lucy. "You take care of yourself, Lucy."

She smiled at him. "I will."

"You still have my card?" Bert asked.

"*Ja*, I've got it," Gabriel said.

"Call if you need anything."

He got out of the car and then, mindful of her injuries, carefully helped Lucy. Once she was steady on her feet, he leaned into the car's open window. "I appreciate it," Gabriel said.

Lucy started toward the house as Bert drove away. As he turned to follow her, he twisted his ankle, sending shooting pain up his left leg. Not wanting to alarm Lucy, he breathed through it. Following behind her, he rubbed his thigh, relieved as it quickly diminished to a burn and then a prickle.

"Would you like something to drink? I have iced tea, lemonade or something hot if you'd prefer," she said as she unlocked the door and stepped inside. He tried not to hobble as he followed her.

"Are you hungry?" he asked, glad his pain had eased. "Would you like me to get some sandwiches?"

"*Danki* but *nay*. I'm not hungry, but I could drink tea."

He stopped and looked around. Almost every available space was filled with baked goods—cakes, pies, bar and regular cookies. "What's all this?"

Looking tired, Lucy ran a hand across her forehead. "Baked goods," she said. "I've arranged to sell them on consignment at King's General Store and Peter's Pockets. I was supposed to deliver these this morning."

"It smells amazing in here," he said. "I'm sure they'll sell well."

"I hope so." Lucy grabbed the teakettle and filled it with water. She shifted to move it to the stove and wobbled unsteadily on her feet.

Gabriel was quick to take it from her hands. "Sit down, *ja*?" he urged gently as he eased her into the nearest chair. "You had an accident. You need to rest. I'll take care of this for you."

"*Danki,*" she whispered, her face pale. She sat and pushed a few of the packaged bakery items out of the way so there was room at the kitchen table for their tea.

Looking at all the cakes and pies and other baked goods, Gabriel realized they would go to waste if they weren't delivered.

"I can take these for you," he offered casually, gesturing with his hand as he leaned back against the counter facing her. The teakettle whistled, and he turned to take it off the heat. "What do you take in your tea?"

When she didn't answer, he looked to find her gaping at him. "What's wrong?"

"Did you just say you'd make my deliveries?"

He hid a grin. "Cups?" he asked, opening cabinet doors. "Here we are." He pulled out two mugs and set them on the counter. "Sugar? Milk?" He faced her.

Lucy hadn't moved. "Why would you offer to make my deliveries?"

"Because you're hurt, and I can." He realized it was true. Because of the scar on his face, he didn't like being around a lot of people. They had a tendency to stare whenever they saw him. He usually made his deliveries early to avoid times when the store was busy, but he would do this for Lucy...because she needed him to. "I make toys and wooden crafts that I sell on consignment, so I understand what you want to do. I have a standing arrangement with both stores, so sit, drink your tea, and then let me do this for you."

He saw her swallow hard. "I don't know what to say." She looked stunned by his offer, which made him feel good.

"How about 'I like sugar in my tea'?"

"Gabriel—"

"Rest, Lucy." He quirked an eyebrow. "Tea bags?"

"In the tin on the counter behind you." She shook her head.

"Milk or cream?"

She scowled. "Just sugar."

Stifling amusement, Gabriel fixed two cups of tea and placed one directly in front of her. He sat down to drink the other one. "As soon as I'm done, I'll start with your deliveries."

* * *

Watching him as he drank from his mug, Lucy shifted uncomfortably in her chair. He had offered to take her baked goods to the stores! She was relieved that everything wouldn't go to waste but she didn't know what to say. Gabriel Fisher, a man she'd never met before today, had rescued her not once but twice. His generosity was beginning to make her feel off-kilter. He would be making her deliveries after rescuing her from her accident, riding with her in the ambulance and staying to accompany her home. After today, she'd figure out a way to cope on her own while she recovered. She couldn't continue to rely on a stranger, even one she thought she could trust.

"Danki," she whispered as she stared into her steaming mug of tea that he'd fixed for her. She took a sip. "It's…*gut*. Just how I like it."

Gabriel's slow smile made her heart beat harder. "Something we have in common. I drink it the same way."

Sipping from her tea, Lucy studied him. He had taken off his hat and set it on the wall hook by the door. Her gaze settled on the scar on his cheek, and it did nothing to take away from his attractive masculine features. Although he was somewhat closed off, she was so comfortable with him that it felt like he was a friend rather than a stranger. She had to remind herself that she didn't know him.

He glanced up suddenly. "You look tired." He narrowed his gaze. "Do you want your pain medicine?"

She shook her head. "I'm fine."

His chair was perpendicular to hers at the table, and Gabriel moved it closer. "You need to relax and let me handle things for you today," he said, his expression intense as he studied her. "Your head hurts, and you've sprained your wrist."

Lucy blushed and averted her gaze. "I've taken too much of your time. I need to learn to manage on my own."

His heavy sigh drew her attention back to his expression. "What bothers you about accepting help? Or is it just mine that bothers you?"

She felt her cheeks heat. *"Nay,"* she whispered. "I'm grateful for your help, but I can't..." Unable to explain, Lucy stared into her teacup. "I asked too much of you already." She thought of her father, a man who should have loved her but clearly didn't.

She trusted Gabriel. He couldn't let her down if she didn't spend more time with him.

"Lucy."

Jerked from her thoughts, she blinked and met Gabriel's gaze. She had the strongest urge to tell him about her past.

"You're in pain." His voice was gentle, reminding her of things she'd once wanted from marriage but would never have now. "I think you should take one pill." He stood as if to get it for her.

"Nay." Lucy shut her eyes against the concern in his gaze.

"Then finish your tea," he quietly urged. "I'll clean up when we're done so you can nap."

"I don't need a nap."

Gabriel stopped to stare at her and Lucy shifted uncomfortably. "Fine," she said. "I'll rest but I doubt I'll sleep."

His small smirk suggested he thought otherwise.

"What time do we need to leave for Susie?" He arched an eyebrow. "You do want her home, *ja*?"

She sighed, resigned to the fact she needed his help. Again. "About six." Lucy couldn't control a yawn and then shot him a glance.

He continued to watch her with amusement. "I'll be back before then. How far do we have to go?"

She hesitated, concerned about what Nancy might say after seeing her with Gabriel. "You don't have to come back. I can get her. If you hitch up my horse for me, I can take my wagon."

A scowl darkened his features. "You cannot steer a wagon safely with a sprained wrist—and you have to be sore after the accident." His lips firmed. "I'll be here by five thirty."

She knew he was right, but she didn't want to admit it. "Gabriel... I appreciate everything you've done, but—"

"I will be here at five thirty," he repeated firmly, his expression brooking no argument. "You can tell me where to go then."

His intent stare made her back off. "Fine, I'll accept your help, but I'll owe you."

They finished their tea in silence. Lucy again fought the urge to learn more about him, about his past. His scar. The stiffness in his gait she'd noticed, as if he'd struggled to walk, when he'd exited Bert's car and approached the house.

Gabriel stood slowly and collected their dishes. "I enjoyed the tea and the company."

Lucy blushed. "Me, too." To her shock, he carried the mugs to the sink to wash. "You are *not* washing the dishes!"

He captured her gaze over his shoulder. "I will because I *want* to. And it's only two mugs." The retort she would have made died on her lips as he filled up the dish basin then washed the mugs before stacking them in the drying rack. She must have made a sound as he reached for a dish towel, because he faced her with narrowed eyes. "Go rest, Lucy," he urged gently. "I'll dry them, pack up your baked goods, and lock up before I leave."

Lucy had to admit that she did feel tired. Now that she'd enjoyed her tea, it seemed as if the morning had caught up with her, and she'd lost all of her energy. She knew her pregnancy often made her tired, but this exhaustion, she realized, was a direct result of the accident.

A dish towel over his shoulder, Gabriel leaned back against the counter with his arms folded and stared at her. "Go lie down, Lucy."

She sighed. *"Oll recht,"* she grumbled. "I'll go upstairs."

His features softened with approval. "I'll be back at five thirty."

She nodded, grateful that he'd offered to get Susie with her. She wanted her little girl home. Susie's smiles and hugs always made her feel better.

As she climbed the stairs wearily, she could visualize Gabriel drying the mugs then putting them away. He amazed her with everything he'd done for her. Harley had never been that helpful, believing that men's and women's work remained separate. She couldn't find it in herself to blame Harley for the way he was—or for anything that had happened in their relationship. Their marriage had been a convenience, and it had gone fairly well, considering Harley had been grieving his late wife when the two of them had wed. About a month before his death, Harley had softened toward her, and Lucy thought their marriage had become something more. They'd grown close enough to conceive a child. But then Harley had become a different person, bitter and riddled with guilt that he'd betrayed the memory of his beloved late wife.

As she settled in bed under the covers, Lucy smiled as she thought again about Gabriel and his rescuing her. It left her wanting to know more about him.

Chapter Three

Lucy had napped, freshened up, eaten a sandwich and was icing her wrist when she heard the sound of buggy wheels on asphalt filter in through an open window. She removed the ice pack and placed it in the freezer to use again later. Opening the door, she watched with a small smile as Gabriel climbed from his vehicle and approached.

His expression was unreadable as he reached her. "Lucy. I hope you were able to rest."

"Too much, I'm afraid. I slept the afternoon away." She stepped back as he walked into the house.

"You needed it. You'll heal more quickly if you get enough sleep." She knew the exact moment when he noticed her Ace bandage on the table. "Shouldn't you be wearing that?"

"I was following the doctor's orders. Icing it to keep the swelling down."

"Do you need any pain medicine?"

Lucy shook her head. "*Nay*, I feel *oll recht*."

His gaze narrowed as he looked at her. "Take the medicine if you are in pain, Lucy. *Please*. Don't wait until you're hurting, because it will be more difficult for the medicine to work if you do."

She widened her eyes at his entreaty. He was acting like he was worried about her. *"Oll recht.* I'll take it if I need it."

Gabriel gave her a nod of approval. "I made your deliveries. Mary King and John Zook were glad to get them. They'll let you know when they need more."

"Danki," she said, blinking rapidly. He had no idea how much he'd helped her by doing that for her. She got herself under control. "If they sell well, then I'll be able to restock and have a good business with them."

"I may be able to help with some of the stores I do business with regularly if you are interested." He didn't wait for her to reply and she was glad, feeling overly emotional. "Are you ready to go?" he asked quietly, as if he'd sensed her mood.

"Ja, I miss my *dochter.* I'm not used to her being gone."

"Let me help you with your Ace bandage." He picked it up, ready to put it on for her.

Lucy shook her head. "I'd rather not wear it. I'll put it on after I get back." She bit her lip. "I don't want to worry them," she said.

His brow cleared. "Let's bring it in case you need it, *ja*?" He picked it up, and she scowled at him, which made him arch an eyebrow.

Minutes later, Gabriel helped her into his buggy then skirted the vehicle to the driver's side. "Where are we headed?" he asked as he climbed in.

Lucy reluctantly gave him the address.

Gabriel flashed her a glance. "What's wrong?"

"Nothing."

"*Lucy.*"

"I don't like taking so much of your time and—"

"And?" He waited for her answer.

"My sister-in-law—"

"You don't know how she'll react to me," he said, his voice flat.

"I'm worried about what she'll say when she sees you with me."

"I guess we'll see," Gabriel murmured, pain flashing briefly in his brown eyes before he flicked the reins and urged the horse pulling his buggy toward the road.

It wasn't his looks that would concern Nancy. It was Nancy's reaction to seeing her brother's widow with another man, someone she'd never met.

The scar across Gabriel's face was raised and jagged, and Lucy realized he must have suffered greatly when he'd gotten hurt. She wanted to know how he'd been hurt, but she didn't feel comfortable asking, since they'd met only that morning.

"Gabriel, this isn't about your scar," she said softly. "'Tis because I'm a widow, and Nancy is my late husband's sister."

He shot her a quick glance but didn't say a word, and she wondered if by mentioning his scar she'd made things worse for him instead of better.

Gabriel could feel the tension rise within him as he guided his horse down the lane leading to Lucy's sister-in-law's property. As the residence came into view, he saw two girls and a boy burst out of the side door, laughing as they ran into the yard. They raced in circles before running up the steps to reenter the house.

His jaw felt tight as he anticipated the children's reactions to his face and the ugly burn scar that marred his left cheek. Seeing adults' reactions was bad enough. Children had a tendency to be outspoken and truthful.

"Stay where you are until I can help you get out," he said brusquely.

"Gabriel." Her tone made him hesitate to study her before climbing down. "I don't want them to know about the accident." She seemed on the verge of tears. *"Please,"* she entreated.

"I understand." And he did. "But I can still help you. No one will think any less of you for accepting help." He kept his tone gentle. "'Tis a simple courtesy."

"My husband never…" She looked away. Finally, she inclined her head in agreement, then gazed through the buggy's windshield, staring toward the house where the children had disappeared.

"He never offered to help you?" he asked with a frown and a quick glance at her baby belly. "But you're—"

Meeting his gaze, Lucy gave him a small smile as she settled a hand over her pregnant belly. "He never knew. I was only a month along, and I didn't even know."

"I'm sorry for your loss."

She looked momentarily startled but then nodded.

Gabriel climbed down and drew a calming breath. Trying to control his increasing anxiety, he tied up his horse and looked around. Horses grazed within the white-fenced paddock. The weather vane on top of the red barn pointing east moved gently with the light breeze. In the distance, he noted a windmill, the blades spinning in slow motion. He circled the buggy and extended a hand to her.

Uncertainty flickered in her expression as, mindful

of her injuries, he carefully helped her down. He immediately released her and turned his attention briefly toward the house.

"Would you like to wait here while I get her?" Lucy asked.

"I will if you want me to."

She exhaled slowly then nodded as if coming to a decision. "I don't mind if you come in with me." She bit her lower lip. "I'd like that, actually."

"Oll recht." Adjusting his hat, he studied the house before turning to Lucy. "Your *dochter* will be happy to see you," he said with a small smile. But not him. More people than not were frightened by his looks. Lizzy, his own betrothed, had broken up with him while he was in the hospital, trying to recover. She'd taken one look at the bright red burn across his face, then at the horrible mass of red, blistered and raw skin along the length of his left leg, and decided that he would never be able to provide for her. He was too injured and damaged to ever farm as planned.

The fire and subsequent breakup had changed him. Mistrustful of love and damaged physically, Gabriel had given up the hope of having a future that included a wife and family. Still, the longing lingered.

Her eyes bright, Lucy approached the house, clearly eager to see her daughter. The door opened again and the two girls he'd seen earlier exited the house, chuckling as they glanced over their shoulders. When the boy appeared at the door, the girls shrieked and raced into the backyard. Gabriel stopped, feeling ill at ease as he waited for Susie to notice them.

The door swung open, and the woman who must be Lucy's sister-in-law stepped outside with a smile. "Susie

will sleep *gut* tonight. They've been running all day."
She frowned slightly when her gaze settled briefly on
Gabriel until the children came back into the side yard,
shrieking and running in circles with the boy chasing
the two girls.

"Nancy, this is Gabriel Fisher," Lucy said, turning
toward him with a smile that warmed him. "He lives
down the street from us."

"Gabriel." Nancy glanced away from his scar to meet
his gaze before looking with curiosity at Lucy.

"Nancy, it seems like Lucy's daughter has been having a *wunderbor* time," Gabriel said, drawing Nancy's
attention.

The woman softened her expression and smiled. "*Ja*,
she's been having fun."

"*Mam!*" Seeing Lucy, Susie grinned and threw herself into her mother's arms. Gabriel saw Lucy wince as
her daughter hugged her hard. "I missed you!"

"I missed you, *dochter*," Lucy murmured. "The *haus*
is not the same without you." She shifted her daughter
to keep her close in a one-armed hug. Her gaze fell on
her niece and softened. "*Hallo*, Sarah." The older girl
nodded in greeting. "It was nice of you to spend the
day with your cousin," she said, her lips curving up
with warmth.

Susie jerked away from her. "You come to take me
home?"

"*Ja*. Are you ready to go?"

Susie bobbed her head as a boy approached and stood
by his mother. She turned and spied Gabriel standing
beside Lucy. "*Hallo*," she greeted, gazing at him with
curiosity. She smiled. "Did you come with my *mudder*?"

"He did," Lucy said, her expression soft. "This is

Gabriel and he's our new neighbor." She smiled in his direction before turning back to her daughter. "Did you have a nice time?"

"*Ja!* Sarah and I played horse, and I got to pick wildflowers in the fields." The little girl grinned. "And then we played tag with Caleb being it!"

"It sounds like you had fun."

"I did, *Mam*. Caleb thought he'd catch me when I ran, but he couldn't!" Susie flashed her cousin an impish look. "Maybe next time." She lowered her voice as she faced them. "I think he is tired, *Mam*. Maybe that's why he can't run as fast as me."

Her gaze gentling, Lucy turned to Nancy's son. "*Hallo*, Caleb."

"Lucy." A little quirk of Caleb's lips told Gabriel that the boy had been humoring his little cousin. Caleb met his gaze, and Gabriel was pleased when Caleb didn't reactive negatively to his facial scar.

Lucy returned her attention to her daughter. "I'm glad you had a *gut* time today." She met Nancy's gaze as she placed her left arm around Susie. "*Danki* for keeping her, *schweschter*."

Nancy didn't answer, because her gaze had settled on Gabriel again before she dragged it away, back to Lucy. "She's a pleasure to have. My *kinner* certainly enjoy when she's visiting." She followed as Lucy and Gabriel moved toward his buggy. "Say *hallo* to Joseph for me," Lucy said.

Susie stared at Gabriel a long moment, then she reached for his right hand. Touched by the child's gesture, Gabriel allowed their fingers to entwine while Lucy did the same with her little girl's other hand. Once close to his vehicle, Gabriel let go of Susie's hand to lift her onto the buggy seat. Then he held out his right hand to Lucy, who grabbed hold and allowed him to help her in, as well.

Susie waved vigorously to Sarah and Caleb. Gabriel noticed that Nancy didn't wave or say a word as he picked up the leathers. She was too busy eyeing them thoughtfully.

"I'll see you at service!" Lucy called out the window.

Nancy smiled. "Bring your upside-down chocolate cake! 'tis Joseph's favorite."

"I will!" Lucy replied loudly.

With the click of his tongue and a flick of the reins, Gabriel steered his horse onto the road. Lucy went silent beside him. He chanced a glance at her and their gazes met. He couldn't tell how she was feeling.

"*Mam*, I'm hungry," Susie said, drawing their attention. "Can I have ice cream?"

Gabriel met Lucy's gaze and whispered, "Brubaker's Creamery isn't far. I'll buy."

"Ice cream sounds *gut*," she murmured, "but I can pay." She hesitated. "I owe you."

He opened his mouth to object, but then closed it again. He didn't argue. There was no point. He'd only upset her, and she'd already suffered a trying day. She shifted in her seat as if she was hurting. "It won't take long," he said, sympathetic to her pain, his pleasure dimming with his concern for her.

She nodded then looked over her shoulder at Susie. "Gabriel is going to take us to a *gut* place for ice cream. We'll get it and bring it home to eat."

In response, Susie clapped her hands and bounced in her seat. "We're getting ice cream!"

"Sit still, *dochter*," Lucy scolded. "You mustn't distract Gabriel's attention from the road. We don't want to have an accident, *ja*?"

"Ja, Mam." Susie sat still, but the grin on Lucy's face as she turned to the front told her that Susie was happy as well as obedient.

Her grin vanished as Lucy locked gazes with him. The memory of her accident earlier hung heavily in the air between them. Gabriel offered her a kind, understanding smile. Recalling her fear and injuries—and the way he'd felt when he'd found her—made the accident a harsh reality, one they wouldn't forget anytime soon.

Later that night Gabriel entered his workshop and set his battery-powered light on his workbench. He loved the smell of wood, sawdust and varnish. He loved working with wood, felt like he was born to woodcraft, and he would never have thought to make a living from a hobby if it hadn't been for the fire. He was supposed to take over the family farm, but the loss of his family, the destruction of the farmhouse and the physical impracticality of farming because of his damaged leg had changed all that. It didn't matter that he couldn't farm. He liked what he did now. *Gott* had gifted him with a skill he enjoyed and the means to earn a living.

Gabriel thought of Susie Schwartz, Lucy's daughter. Her innocent acceptance of him had tugged at his heart. He wanted to make something special for the little girl, and he needed better light than the diminishing daylight. Despite all that had happened that day, he'd enjoyed his time with her and Lucy when they'd eaten ice cream earlier. Susie had chosen the creamery's triple chocolate flavor, and he loved the way chocolate had lined her little mouth while she ate. He'd chosen rocky road, and Lucy had eaten chocolate chip mint. Several times he and Lucy exchanged smiles over Susie's antics. Lucy's daughter was a warm, loving child, and it made Gabriel happy yet sad for himself, that he'd never enjoy one of his own.

He picked up a piece of basswood and eyed it carefully then set it down. Catching sight of a block of birch, Gabriel knew what he wanted to do. He'd make Susie a waddling duck toy from birch, pine and basswood.

Suddenly, a shooting pain hit his thigh, and he cried out. Gasping, eyes tearing, he grabbed onto the stool near his workbench and sat down. He rubbed the scarred flesh, hoping for relief. He knew he'd overdone it today with Lucy's rescue and then remaining constantly on the move. It had been six months since the pain had been this bad.

In the first months he'd been released from the hospital after the fire, he'd suffer an attack in the evening or middle of the night after too much activity. For the last six months, he'd no longer suffered the unbearable stabbing pains that wore him out, enduring only paresthesia—the sensation of pins and needles that felt more manageable to him. The progress had made him sure that his leg was improving. Until now.

When the sharp pain didn't subside, Gabriel gave up trying to work and gingerly got down from the stool, stumbling as his pain worsened. He fumbled for his lantern and staggered out of his shop then hobbled, crying out with each step he took until he finally reached the house. "Emily!"

His sister looked up from the kitchen table where she was mending one of his shirts, her frown immediately turning to an expression of concern as she saw him through the screen door.

"Ach nay, bruder!" She sprang up to open the door and helped him into a chair, then grabbed a second chair to prop up both of his legs. Without another word, she went to a cabinet and pulled out a bottle of over-the-counter medication.

"That's not going to help," he said through gritted teeth.

"Take it anyway, Gabriel," she cried, her green eyes filling with tears. *"Please!* It certainly can't hurt." She shoved two pills and a glass of water at him, watching as he took the medicine. "What else can we do?"

"I don't know," he gasped. Gabriel rubbed his thigh, grimacing as he massaged the scarred tissue. Rubbing it didn't help this time, but he didn't know what else to do.

Emily spun and grabbed two dish towels from a drawer. She wet the tea towel under cold water from the faucet, then hurried back to Gabriel. "Do you want me to cut your pant leg?" she asked, clearly upset.

"Nay, I don't want to ruin them."

After a nod, his sister lay the wet tea towel lengthwise over the tri-blend fabric covering the worst area of his damaged leg, from his thigh to his knee. "I don't know if this will help," she murmured.

With a groan, he released his leg, leaning forward to bury his head in his hands, praying for the pain to stop. Because it hurt so badly now, he knew his muscles would continue to be sore afterward. His leg was scarred and ugly under his clothes, but he could live with the way it looked. It wasn't as if anyone would see it anyway. But this type of pain was unbearable—a reminder of everything he'd lost during the fire that had stolen family from him and Emily. A reminder that he was a damaged man. The fire still gave him nightmares, although those had gotten a little better since they'd moved to New Berne.

"What else can I do?" Emily eyed him with concern.

He opened his eyes, leaned back in his chair. "Nothing. You know how it is. It will eventually ease on its own." And praise the Lord, it was easing. The sharpness of the pain had morphed into a dull throb and then the familiar burning sensation of pins and needles.

"I thought you were over this," Emily said. "Maybe we should ask the doctor for pain medicine—"

"Nay." Gabriel knew the pills wouldn't help. By the time the medicine got into his system, the pain usually had diminished already. He'd needed the pills during his second-degree burn treatments and again after his surgeries, and the medication had helped then. "'Tis *oll recht*, Em. 'Tis getting better."

Emily closed her eyes briefly, and when she opened them again, he saw relief in them, but it was mingled with deep concern. Her expression was one he knew only too well after seeing it enough times after he was released from the hospital.

"Maybe you need to see the neurologist," she said. "There could be a new treatment available."

He nodded. "I'll stop by to make an appointment in the morning."

She jerked a nod. *"Gut."* She picked up the wet towel and placed the dry terry cloth one over the area to soak up the dampness. "I know it didn't help much, but I had to do something," she said quietly. "And maybe the ibuprofen will help with your sore muscles now that the worst has passed."

Gabriel reached out to grab her hand. "I appreciate what you did." He managed a small smile. "We'll both sleep well tonight," he stated, hoping that it was true.

"Ja." She squeezed the wet tea towel over the sink. "I can take you to Dr. Jorgensen's office to schedule your appointment tomorrow morning if you'd like."

"Nay. I'll be fine by then. If I'm not, I'll let you take me."

Emily smiled weakly. "Make sure you do."

He gently eased his leg off the chair. "I think I'll head to bed." He struggled to rise and was glad to find the worst of the pain was gone.

"You'll sleep downstairs tonight," she told him.

He nodded. He didn't want to do anything that might aggravate his leg. He started toward the great room and the small bed he'd made. He slept downstairs whenever he was too tired or sore to go up to his bedroom.

"Gabriel?" Emily's voice stopped him. "I think you've been doing too much, making those deliveries yesterday. Maybe 'tis time to think about opening your own shop. You've been wanting to. Why wait? We still have some of the money from selling the farm, *ja?*"

"Ja, but—"

"No buts, it's time to look for a place. Or you could sell your things right from the *haus?* Think about it, *ja?*"

"I'll think about it," he promised. Since he'd turned his woodworking skills into making money for them, he'd envisioned eventually opening his own shop. Emily's suggestion that he sell his crafts right from home might work. It would certainly help with the problem of having to make deliveries to area merchants. But he didn't want strangers in his home, nor did he want them in his shop. Which meant he'd have to build a separate building or convert part of his barn where he and Emily could handle customers.

Working and selling close to home would be ideal for him, but he wasn't sure he was ready to invest the rest of the money they'd gotten from selling the farm property. There wasn't much. It was a blessing that he had any of it left. His Amish community in Ohio had been wonderful in helping with his medical bills, but he'd still paid a good share. Would it be wise to use the rest of the money? What if something went wrong with his leg again and he ended up in the hospital? It throbbed painfully, reminding him of the horrible weeks of burn care and failed surgeries until finally, months later, the skin grafts had taken.

As his mind tried to settle into a dark place, Gabriel forced himself to remember this morning when he'd helped Lucy. If faced with the same situation, he would carry her from the buggy again. Some things were worth suffering for afterward.

The next morning, he drove to the medical center and made an appointment. There'd been a cancellation, and he'd be seeing Dr. Jorgensen next Monday.

As soon as he got home, Gabriel returned to his workshop. He was feeling better, but the dull ache in his leg reminded him to take it easy. He set the supplies he needed on his workbench then pulled his stool closer so he could work. When he'd delivered Lucy's bakery items yesterday, both store owners had asked for more of his wooden toys and crafts.

Putting the idea of Susie's toy aside for now, he sat down and got to work. He decided to build two toy rocking horses, using the wood he'd brought home from the lumberyard yesterday. The rocking horses were popular with English customers. He cut out pieces for the heads, the bodies and the curved rails that would make them rock. He then sanded each piece of wood until he was pleased with their smoothness. Two hours later, he finished putting both horses together with dowels and wood glue. Tomorrow he'd paint on the eyes and mouth and add small pieces of leather for the ears and yarn for the mane and tail.

Gabriel looked around the workshop for material to decide what else to make. There was enough wood for a couple of birdhouses and a small shelf or two. He climbed off his stool and carefully reached for the wood, grabbing hold of one plank of pine. The muscles in his leg protested and stiffened to the point of pain. He huffed out a groan and straightened with wood in hand. He set it on his workbench and closed his eyes as he took a moment to focus on relaxing his seized leg.

"Gabriel!" His sister burst into the room, startling him, nearly making him tumble over.

He gasped and righted himself. "Emily! Can't you enter a room without scaring me to death?"

Emily frowned. "I'm sorry."

He softened. "What's wrong?"

"Nothing. I wanted to let you know that I've invited someone special to supper Thursday evening."

Two nights from now. He frowned. "Who?"

"His name is Aaron Hostetler, and I like him. A lot."

He hesitated before replying. His sister had a beau? He knew that someday Emily would marry and leave him, but he didn't want to think about that now. He told himself to stop worrying. He was getting ahead of himself. "How long have you known him?"

Emily blushed. "A few weeks?" She blinked. "*Oll recht*, almost a month."

Gabriel raised his eyebrows. They'd only moved here two months ago. He drew a calming breath. It was just supper, he reminded himself. He managed a smile. "I look forward to meeting him."

"What shall I cook?" she asked, suddenly looking agitated. "I don't know what to cook!"

He closed the distance between them and reached for his sister's hands. "If this man is interested in you, then he will love anything you make because you made it for him." He eyed her with affection as he released her. "I'm partial to your chicken potpie."

Tugging on her *kapp* string, she brightened. "Do you think he'll like it?"

"Your chicken potpie is the best I've ever eaten. I think you have nothing to worry about."

"I'll make that, then," Emily said with a smile. She spun and started to leave his workshop then halted. "And I'll bake lemon cake for dessert."

"Em!" he called as she ran toward the door. "What time is it?"

"'Tis half past two," she said.

Gabriel frowned as he watched Emily leave. He'd been so involved with the work he was unaware of how much time had passed.

Thursday afternoon Emily would want his help before her beau's arrival. He knew his sister well enough to tell she was worried that he and her new beau wouldn't get along. But Gabriel was prepared to look kindly on the man as long as Aaron didn't mistreat his sister and his feelings for Emily were genuine.

Emily was his only surviving family and she meant

the world to him. Since they'd moved here, he'd been content to earn a living so he could take care of his sister.

But something odd had happened to him since Lucy's accident. He felt…drawn to the pretty widow. He'd made a friend. He should stop in to see how she was doing.

It bothered him that he missed seeing her after only one day. His leg was a problem for him, but that didn't mean he couldn't enjoy a friendship with her and her daughter. Being friends was fine, he decided. He could avoid friends when his pain—and his nightmares—got out of hand.

Thinking about mother and daughter had him eager to check in with them. Lucy was pretty, a wonderful mother and someone with a good heart. And Susie was a delight. Clearly unbothered by his face, Susie had smiled at him frequently while they'd eaten ice cream. He was glad to know they were his neighbors. He could head over to see them. If they were busy, he'd leave.

Friendly neighbors, he could do.

Chapter Four

"*Mam*, why is that on your hand?" Susie asked as Lucy re-pinned her child's long blond hair after a busy morning of Susie playing outside. The little girl's prayer *kapp* had long been tossed aside during her daughter's antics. She'd stood and spun until she got dizzy and fell, only to do it all over again. Was it any wonder her dress had become soiled and her hair a mess? *"Mam?"*

Last night Lucy had rewrapped her wrist after her daughter had gone to bed. She'd managed to make breakfast without the Ace bandage, but her wrist had started to ache afterward. "I hurt it, but it's getting better. This keeps me from bumping it again."

Her child glanced up at her, her blue eyes filled with concern. "I'm sorry you got hurt."

"I know you are, *dochter*," she said with affection. She tugged playfully on a lock of Susie's hair.

"When did you bump it?"

"Yesterday."

Susie looked puzzled but didn't ask how. Lucy was relieved.

"Turn around, *dochter*, so I can finish fixing your

hair." With the bandage wrapped around her wrist more firmly, she could more easily manage a few chores. Lucy continued to brush her daughter's golden locks, then pulled her hair into a bun and secured it with hairpins. She didn't bother with Susie's head covering. Today was wash day and she would wash her daughter's *kapp* and dress with the rest of their garments before she hung them to dry on the clothesline in her backyard. She decided to throw her *kapp* in the wash as well and took it off, replacing it with her black kerchief.

"Can we see Gabriel today?" Susie asked as she descended the stairs slowly, her bare feet silent on them.

"I don't think so, Susie. He is probably busy today," Lucy said as they reached the bottom. She was amazed how quickly her daughter had taken to Gabriel.

"He's our neighbor. If he's not busy, he can come over?" Her little girl gazed at her hopefully as they entered the kitchen.

"*Ja*, if he's not busy, but we can't expect him." Lucy settled her daughter in a chair and pushed her closer to the table. "Do you want a sandwich?"

Susie wiggled in her chair. "Can I have cornflakes for lunch?" She grinned while Lucy fixed her cereal with milk and set it before her. "Can we visit Gabriel if he doesn't come here?"

"I don't know, *dochter*." She had mixed feelings about seeing Gabriel again. She'd missed him since he'd left last evening, but she couldn't expect him to visit just because she wanted him to. *He is my neighbor*, she reminded herself. *And I'm grateful for all he's done*. What if she made him a treat to thank him? They could stop briefly by his house and deliver it. "Shall we make him a pie?"

"*Ja!* A chocolate pie!" Susie exclaimed, smacking the table in her excitement. "And we can bring it to him!"

Lucy nodded. "We can bring it to him, but that doesn't mean we'll stay." She knew where Gabriel lived. He'd pointed his house out to her as they passed it when he'd taken her and Susie home after ice cream.

While Susie ate, Lucy checked to see if she had everything she needed for the pie. Thankfully she did, so there was no reason to go to the store.

Three hours later, Lucy pulled a pie shell from the oven. She had sent Susie upstairs an hour ago to play quietly in her room after her child had become whiny while rolling out the pie dough. She'd checked on Susie a half hour ago and found her asleep in her bed, and Lucy had completed some household chores.

With the pie crust cooling on the rack on the counter, she assembled the ingredients for the filling, added them into a saucepan on the stove and stirred them together as they heated.

A loud knock on her door drew her attention. Lucy widened her eyes when she saw her late husband's best friend, Aaron Hostetler. "Aaron."

"*Hallo*, Lucy," he greeted with a smile. "May I come in?"

"*Ja.*" She pushed open the door and stepped back to allow him entry. He tugged off his hat and set it on her kitchen table. "Susie's fallen asleep," she told him. "She spent the day running with her cousins yesterday, and she's still tired."

Aaron's expression softened at the mention of her daughter. "I'm sure Sarah and Caleb kept her busy."

Lucy averted her gaze as she nodded. "*Ja*, they did." The mixture in the saucepan on the stove started to boil.

She rushed to turn off the burner, stirring the contents several times, and decided it was thick enough. She removed it from the stove and set it on a hot mat on the counter. "I'm in the middle of making a pie."

"Smells *gut*," he said. She turned, startled that he stood so close behind her. She must have gasped because he instantly stepped back.

"Special occasion?" he asked as she faced him.

"I'm making the pie for my neighbor." Lucy turned back to stir the chocolate cream before she dumped it into the baked pie shell. "Is there something you needed?"

"I just wanted to stop by."

"And so you did." She hoped her smile took the sting out of her reply.

He grew quiet, and she realized that something on the counter caught his attention. Her elastic bandage. She'd taken it off to work with the pie dough and forgotten to put it back on.

"What's that?" Aaron asked, his eyes widening.

"It's an Ace bandage. I use it for support while I'm doing chores."

His face turned pale. "It's not because of…"

She gaped at him. *"Nay."* She knew he was remembering the scar on her left arm.

Aaron looked relieved, which made her wonder why. "I should go. Will you tell Susie I stopped by?" He suddenly seemed anxious to leave.

Lucy managed a smile. "I will."

He grabbed his hat from the kitchen table and pulled open the door. "If you need anything…"

"I won't, but *danki*."

After taking two steps out the door, he turned to face her. "Lucy—"

"I am fine, Aaron. You need to stop feeling responsible for me—for us."

As soon as he'd left, Lucy released a sharp breath. Aaron had been a good friend during the weeks after Harley's death, she thought as she poured the chocolate cream into the pie shell, but she needed him to stop his worrying and move on with his life. She and Susie were fine.

It was late afternoon when Gabriel drove his buggy the half mile to Lucy's. If it weren't for his leg, he'd walk. It was a beautiful day for it. With each click of horse hooves against pavement, he felt his heart lighten at the prospect of seeing her again.

He frowned when he saw a man in a wagon leaving her property up ahead. Gabriel slowed his gelding. Who was that? he wondered, a sinking sensation setting in his chest. Probably the husband of a friend or neighbor. As he reached her driveway, he stepped on the brake before making the turn. After parking his vehicle close to the barn, he tied up his horse. Doubts crept in as he approached the house. He worried about being welcome—after all, they'd only met the day before. *But seeing if she is oll recht is the neighborly thing to do*, he reassured himself.

Heart racing, Gabriel raised his hand to the side door and knocked softly. His first thought as he waited for her to notice him was to ask her about the man, but he wouldn't because it was none of his business if she had a male visitor.

The interior door was open, leaving only the screen

door between him and inside. Shifting slightly, he leaned in and saw Lucy putting dishes in the sink. She hadn't heard him.

"Lucy?" he called softly as he knocked again.

She stiffened and faced the door. Her expression brightened when she saw him. "Gabriel, I didn't expect to see you today." She wiped her hands on a patchwork cooking apron as she approached with joy in her pretty blue eyes. "Come in."

"How are you feeling?" he asked, regarding her with concern as he pulled open the door and entered. The rich smell of chocolate permeated the air, making his mouth water.

"A little sore, but I'm managing."

He studied her carefully. "You're not overdoing it, are you?"

"*Nay*, I'm just doing what needs to be done."

Gabriel nodded. *"Gut."* He paused. "I just wanted to see how you were doing."

She gestured toward the kitchen table. "Have a seat. Susie's been napping but I need to wake her. If she sleeps too long, she won't when it's bedtime."

He took off his hat and hung it on a wall hook.

After a glance toward the counter, she met his gaze. "I'll be right back. Can I get you something to drink first?"

Gabriel shook his head and then watched as she left the room. He absently fingered the raised scar on his cheek as he listened to Lucy's soft footsteps on the stairs. Within moments, he smiled at the sound of a little girl's excited voice accompanied by the calm tone of her mother's as they came down the stairs.

Susie burst into the room ahead of her *mam*. "Ga-

briel! You're here!" Her pale blue eyes lit up as soon as she saw him.

"*Hallo*, Susie." He flashed her a grin. "It's nice to see you again." Narrowing his gaze, he studied her thoughtfully. "Have you gotten taller since I last saw you?"

"Nay!" She laughed. "I can't grow in one day!"

Amused, Gabriel arched an eyebrow. "Are you sure?"

The child bobbed her head. Susie sniffed the air, her little nose wrinkling as she faced her mother. "I smell chocolate. You finished it?"

Her gaze settling on him, Lucy nodded. "Gabriel, I made you a pie. I haven't had a chance to chill it yet. I hope you like chocolate cream."

Stunned, he could only look from her to the pie on the kitchen counter and back again. "You made me a pie?"

Her eyes sparkling with happiness, she inclined her head. "It's a thank-you for…" She blushed then looked quickly at her daughter. "You know."

"Lucy, you didn't have to do that. You don't owe me anything—" He stopped when he realized that Susie watched their exchange with curiosity.

"Don't you like chocolate pie?" Susie asked, her pale blue eyes wide with innocence.

"I love it, especially chocolate cream pie," he said, his lips curving.

"Gut!" the little girl cried. "'Cause it's *de-lish-us*!" She turned to her mother. *"Mam*, can I have a snack to hold me until supper?"

"Ja, if you'd like." She turned to Gabriel. "Would you like some tea and cookies?" she asked, her lips twitching with amusement.

"I would. *Danki*," he said, surprising himself. He'd

only planned to stay a few minutes, but the only place he wanted to be right now was here in Lucy Schwartz's house, enjoying a snack with her and her daughter.

She placed the pie in the refrigerator. When she reached into the pantry, probably for the cookies, Gabriel got up and put on the teakettle.

Her eyes widened when she saw what he had done. "Gabriel—"

"'Tis fine, Lucy." The teakettle whistled. He poured the hot water into two mugs and added tea bags while she opened a container and put cookies on a plate. Gabriel added sugar to the mugs then brought them to the table.

Lucy poured Susie a glass of milk. She raised her eyebrows when Susie grabbed a cookie and dunked it in her milk.

Her daughter shrugged. "I saw Caleb do it, and I wondered if it tasted better." Susie took a bite. "It does," she mumbled through a mouthful of cookie.

Gabriel snickered; he couldn't help himself. Lucy locked gazes with him, her expression filled with good humor.

He ate bites of cookie between sips of tea. The cookies were tasty. Chocolate chip, his favorite.

Susie talked nonstop. "When did you move here? Do you have family living with you?"

He managed to keep calm although personal questions usually alarmed him, but this was Susie, an innocent child with no bad intentions. "I moved here two months ago, and my sister Emily lives with me."

"I don't have a sister, but I might soon! Or a *bruder*. I don't care which one we get."

She drank from her milk and ate another bite of

cookie, swallowing before she continued asking questions. "Do you have any animals? A dog or a cat? I like dogs and cats," Susie said.

"Dochter," Lucy said firmly. "That's enough questions for Gabriel."

Susie nodded, clearly unoffended. She finished two cookies silently and drank all of her milk. She wore a milk mustache when she set down her cup. Lucy chuckled as she wiped her daughter's mouth with a napkin. "Can I get down?" Susie asked.

Her mother nodded. "Where are you going?"

Her little girl smiled secretly before she approached Gabriel and crawled into his lap. She patted his cheek. Susie's fingers moved to caress his scar. "You hurt yourself."

He stiffened, but only for a second, as the child looked at him with genuine concern. *"Ja."*

"I can fix it," she said sweetly. To his astonishment, she leaned forward and kissed his scarred cheek. When she pulled back, she was smiling. "There! Now it won't hurt so much. *Mam* always kisses my boo-boos better."

Emotion rolled over him in thick waves. He fell instantly in love with Lucy's daughter. *"Danki*, Susie."

"You're *willkomm*," she replied breezily as she climbed down from his lap. She kissed her mother. "Can I play outside for a little while?"

Lucy gazed at her daughter as if surprised by Susie's kindness, but she looked happy that her child was open and loving to a man she barely knew yet obviously cared about. "Why don't you play in your room? We'll go outside together after supper."

The child nodded. "I'll see you later, Gabriel. I liked eating cookies with you." Susie scampered from the room.

Silence fell once Susie was gone. Averting her gaze, Lucy rose and awkwardly piled up their plates.

He stopped her with a gentle touch on her arm. "Lucy?"

She seemed to freeze but she met his gaze head-on. *"Danki."* Wondering if she could read his thoughts, he quietly studied her. "Your *dochter*…she has a beautiful *hartz.*"

Lucy blinked rapidly but managed a smile that looked genuine. "I am blessed to have her in my life."

He nodded. "I can understand that," he whispered, holding her gaze. The tension in the room was thick. It wasn't an angry tension but an awareness between a man and a woman. Worried by the feeling, Gabriel stood. "I enjoyed the snack and…" *the time we spent together.* "I should go and leave you to your afternoon."

She rose. "I'm glad you stopped by," she said as he grabbed his hat from a wall hook and settled it on his head. She stopped him with a touch on his arm as he opened the door to leave. "Gabriel, your pie." She retrieved it from the refrigerator and brought it to him.

He gave her a wry grin as he took it from her. "Can't leave it behind when it's my favorite."

"Be careful with it or it may spill. Another hour in the refrigerator will help."

As he left her house, Gabriel felt as if his heart had taken a wallop. He liked Lucy and he liked her daughter. Maybe too much. He set the pie carefully on the front floor of his buggy before he climbed in.

He was touched by Lucy's gesture. Closing his eyes,

he thought of the young widow and her daughter and felt a longing for something he would never have. He couldn't allow himself to be vulnerable again. He was a broken man and he had to keep some distance between them. With a sigh, he reminded himself that he and Lucy were neighbors and possibly now friends, but he could never allow them to become anything more.

Chapter Five

Two days after Gabriel's visit, Lucy sat at the table with Susie, watching her daughter drawing pictures with crayons. "Why don't you draw a picture of a duck like the ones we saw last week in the pond?" she asked when her daughter seemed to struggle with what to draw.

With the tip of her little tongue showing between her lips, Susie concentrated on her drawing for several minutes. She stared at what she'd drawn and frowned. "*Mam*, can I draw in my room? This is going to take a while."

Lucy hid a smile. "*Ja, dochter.* Don't get crayon on the floor or furniture," she warned and grinned as Susie grabbed the crayons and all the paper Lucy had given her and ran from the room.

"*Hallo!*" a feminine voice called through the screened door.

"*Hallo?*" Lucy was startled to see a group of three women she recognized from church, although she couldn't remember their names. "What a nice surprise." She opened the door wide to allow them inside, stepping back as they entered. These women had never visited before, not that she'd enjoyed interaction with the community women while Harley was alive. He'd never allowed them to stay for the midday meal after service or to visit anyone but his sister's family.

"Tea?" she asked. Each woman wanted a cup, so Lucy put on the teakettle then turned to face them.

"We'd like to invite you to my *haus* on Visiting Day," a young woman with red hair and blue eyes said. She looked as if she was in her midtwenties. "I'm Rachel King."

"Are you related to the Kings of King's General Store?" Lucy asked.

"My in-laws." Rachel pulled out a chair at the kitchen table.

The other women shifted the table out from the wall and they sat down. The teakettle whistled. Lucy removed it from the burner and poured out four cups of hot water, which she brought to the table. She set out the fixings for tea and a plate of cookies for the women to snack on.

"I'm Margaret Troyer," a slightly older woman said once Lucy took her seat. "But everyone calls me Maggie. My husband is church deacon."

While she didn't know many church members well, Lucy was aware of each of the elders. "Deacon Thomas."

"Ja." A small, secret smile curved her naturally pink lips.

"'Tis nice of you to visit," Lucy said, wondering why they had.

Rachel chuckled. "We're widows. Well, we were, but not anymore." She pulled the sugar bowl closer and put a spoonful into her tea. "We'd like you to join our 'widows who aren't widows' group, Lucy. We know things have been hard for you, but we'll help you find a better life. There are other men out there. Like us, you will marry again one day to someone who will make a *gut* husband, who will care for you and Susie—" she gestured toward Lucy's belly "—and your little one."

"I appreciate your visit, but I don't know if I'm ready," Lucy admitted, dreading their reaction. She wasn't sure she'd ever be ready.

Each of three women smiled. "We're here," the third one said, "because there's been talk about the other women in our community insisting you need a husband since you have a little one on the way. We're here to support you." She grinned. "I'm Hannah Brubaker. My husband and I own Brubaker's Creamery."

"We understand that you're still grieving," Maggie said before Lucy had a chance to respond to Hannah. "You have time. We remember what it was like after losing our husbands. There's no reason for the others to press you to wed." She exchanged looks with Rachel. "We'd like to be your friends." She paused to take a sip from her tea. "Service is at our house on Sunday. We're hosting."

Lucy hesitated, deciding that it would be nice to have their friendship even if she never married again. "I can make dessert."

"Wunderbor!" Hannah exclaimed. "Bring that for Visiting Day at Rachel's, too. We've tasted your desserts." She grabbed a cookie from a plate Lucy had put on the table. "I recently bought one of your cakes. It was delicious." She took a bite of the cookie. "This is tasty! I wish I could bake like this. I'm a terrible baker."

Her eyes widened at the woman's admission. Lucy didn't know how to respond.

"Your desserts have been selling well," Rachel said. "Mary will get in touch with you soon to ask for more."

Lucy smiled, pleased.

Now that they'd made their intentions known, the churchwomen chatted about their families and the community as they drank their tea and ate cookies. After an hour, they stood and took their leave. Lucy stood on the stoop, waving, and watched as the women left together in Hannah's buggy. After the vehicle disappeared from sight, she turned toward the house. The sound of carriage wheels behind her made her stop and turn around.

"Lucy." Gabriel's familiar voice made her smile. She waited as he tied up his horse before he headed in her direction. Seeing Gabriel Fisher gave her a thrill and made her realize how much she liked his company.

He approached, his expression serious as he reached her. "I heard from Eli Lapp about your buggy. He left a message at King's General Store. He wants to talk with you about it."

"Did he say how much?" When he shook his head, she asked, "When does he want me to call?"

"As soon as possible. I have his number. We can go whenever you're ready." He pushed back his hat brim, and she could see into the shiny depths of his dark brown eyes. "Where's Susie?" he asked.

"Playing in her room." Feeling suddenly breathless, she pressed a hand to her throat. "Are you sure you have time?"

He tugged on his left earlobe. *"Ja."*

Hearting beating wildly, she turned to open the door. "Come in while I get her."

He held on to the doorframe and waited as she entered first. Lucy was conscious of him behind her, his nearness, his scent and the even sound of his breathing. She was drawn to Gabriel as she'd never been drawn to another man. It somehow felt right to be in his company. She caught her breath as she locked gazes with this kind, striking man.

"Have a seat," she said, and then hurried upstairs to Susie's room. Her heart thundered in her chest when she reached the top landing, but not because of the run. Her racing heart was her reaction to the attractive man downstairs in her kitchen.

Lucy smiled as she entered her daughter's room. "Gabriel is here—"

"Gabriel!" Susie didn't wait to hear any more. She flew out of the room and thundered down the stairs in her eagerness to see him.

Susie had left the drawings she'd done on the floor. Lucy picked them up and set them on her daughter's bed. She went downstairs to find her daughter at the table talking a mile a minute with Gabriel intently listening to everything she had to say.

"I drew a duck," she told him. "*Mam* gave me paper and crayons so I can draw things. *Ach nay!*" With a frown, she climbed down from her chair. "I drew something for you, Gabriel, but I left it in my room!" She saw her mother standing in the doorway. "*Mam*, do I have time to get his picture?"

Lucy met Gabriel's amused gaze. "Does she?" she asked him with a little twitch of her lips as she hid a smile.

"*Ja*, we have time."

With a relieved cry, Susie ran up the stairs, and seconds later, they heard her little feet clopping down again. She approached him, clutching a sheet of paper. "Here, Gabriel. I hope you like it." She thrust the paper at him then climbed onto the chair next to him.

Gabriel spread it carefully on the tabletop. Lucy leaned close to get a look and saw a house with three people in the yard—a man, a woman and a little girl. She saw him blink and swallow hard several times as he studied it, as though deeply moved. Lucy, understanding what the drawing meant, was shocked.

"Do you like it?" Susie asked worriedly. "It's you, *Mam* and me outside."

Smiling, he reached out to touch her cheek. "I love it. It's *wunderbor.*"

She grinned. *"Gut!"* She got down from the chair. "Where are we going?"

"King's General Store," Lucy said as she straightened her daughter's *kapp*. "I need to make a phone call."

Susie pulled away. "Can I get a candy bar?"

"Susan Schwartz! *Nay*, you may not have a candy bar," she scolded. "You don't get one every time we go into a store."

Her daughter made a face. "Why not?"

"Because it's simply not done!"

"Just this one time, *Mam*?" Big light blue eyes pleaded as Susie looked up at her, her lower lip quivering after her mother's scolding. "I won't ask next time."

Lucy sighed, hating to disappoint her daughter. "This one last time. You're not to ask for any again."

Susie grinned, displaying little white teeth. She turned to Gabriel. "Do you like candy bars?"

Gabriel nodded, and there was laughter in his brown eyes. She shook her head but soon found herself silently laughing along with him. Apparently, he didn't think her a terrible mother for giving in.

"Let's go, *dochter*, before it gets too late."

"It's still light outside," Susie said. "There is plenty of time."

Gabriel coughed into his sleeve, and Lucy knew he was trying to control his amusement. Finally, with a straight face, he stood and held up the drawing. "Do I get to keep this?" he asked Susie gently.

"*Ja*, I drew it for you."

"*Danki*, Susie."

The child nodded. "You're *willkomm*." She opened the door and skipped outside toward Gabriel's buggy.

Silence filled the room after Susie had left the house. "You are truly blessed, Lucy," Gabriel said, his voice filled with emotion. "You have a beautiful, loving child."

"I know," she said, unwilling to look away from the raw pain she suddenly glimpsed in his expression. She resisted the urge to reach out to comfort him.

He gave her a small smile and opened the door, allowing her to leave before he followed. "You have your key?" When Lucy nodded, he turned the lock then pulled the door shut behind him.

Her throat was tight as Lucy walked with him to his vehicle. Susie had already crawled inside. Gabriel offered his hand and she clasped it firmly as he helped her in. How could she not like him? Gabriel was kind and considerate, a genuinely caring man. And he seemed to adore her daughter.

After a short journey to King's General Store, Gabriel got out, tied up his horse and helped her then Susie out of the buggy. He gave Lucy the note with Eli Lapp's phone number. She entered the store ahead of Gabriel, who followed with Susie holding his hand. Lucy was amazed at the easy way her daughter gravitated toward him. Lucy hadn't needed the peek at Susie's drawing to realize how much her daughter adored him.

She thought of Rachel, Hannah and Maggie. Would she find happiness with another man like her new friends had?

Lucy greeted Mary King with a smile before she went to the pay phone in the back of the store. Pulling several coins from a money purse stashed beneath the waistband of her apron, Lucy dropped them into the slot and dialed Eli's number. The phone rang three times before he picked up.

"Lapp's Carriage Shop. Eli speaking."

Gabriel could see Lucy on the phone. Her brow was furrowed as she listened to whatever Eli was saying. Eventually, she hung up the phone then looked around as if searching for him and Susie. She found them in the candy aisle. It was no surprise that Susie had grabbed an entire pack of chocolate bars.

"So we can share," Susie said as she held up the package to show her mother.

"Did you talk with Eli?" Gabriel asked softly while Susie sorted through the other candy on the shelf.

Lucy nodded. "He said he could have it finished for me by the middle of next week."

He studied her, noting her distress, and shifted closer. "Does it cost too much?"

"I have enough," she assured him. "Although I have a few places I need to go before Eli will have it ready for me. As long as it doesn't rain, I'll be fine taking my wagon."

He hesitated. "I'm not sure that's a *gut* idea, Lucy. Not with your sprained wrist." He scratched above his left eyebrow with his finger. "Where do you need to go?"

"Church is this Sunday. The Troyers are hosting. I can't miss it."

Gabriel stayed silent as he debated whether or not it was time for him to become an active member of this Amish community. He could go, as long as his leg held up. "I'll be happy to take you to church service."

She raised her eyebrow. "You will?"

He inclined his head. "I haven't attended church here yet. If you and Susie don't mind riding with me, it will be my pleasure to take you."

Her gaze softened. "*Danki.* I'd appreciate that."

"*Gut.*" He glanced over his shoulder and smiled as he faced her again. "Your *dochter* can't make up her mind about the candy she wants."

"And why did I tell her she could have any?"

Gabriel chuckled. "Because she knows exactly what to say to convince you."

"I'll take care of this," she said. "It's getting late and we haven't had supper yet." She marched toward her daughter and grabbed the bag of chocolates Susie had chosen first. "Time to go, little one. These will have to do." Catching Susie by the hand, she went to the front register and paid Mary for the candy. When she was done, she turned and saw his anxious look. "What's wrong?"

"I forgot we're having company to supper. I need to get home."

Lucy blushed. "I'm sorry. It's not that far. Susie and I can walk."

He frowned. "*Nay*, your *haus* is on my way home."

He followed as she hurried Susie to the buggy and waited for her to get in. Gabriel got to Susie first, picked her up and set her in the back seat. He frowned when Lucy didn't wait for his help. She climbed into the front seat and he got in beside her. "I'm sorry it took us so long."

"It didn't, Lucy. I was having a nice time. And I simply forgot my sister invited a guest to supper."

Gabriel pulled into her driveway a few minutes later. Worried about being late, he jumped out to help her and Susie climb down and was back in the driver's seat within seconds. He waved before he picked up the leathers. "I'll see you soon, Lucy. Be a *gut girl* for your *mam*, Susie."

"I will, Gabriel." Her daughter tore open the pack of chocolates and pulled out four candy bars. "Wait!" Susie cried when the carriage rolled forward. Gabriel immediately drew back on the reins. "Here. For after supper," she told him.

His eyes were soft as he accepted the candy. "*Danki*, Susie." He turned to Lucy. "Have a nice night."

And then with a wave and a flick of the reins, he was heading home, feeling bad that he had to leave them too quickly.

Chapter Six

Hurrying home, Gabriel urged his horse into a trot. He'd wanted to stay with Lucy and Susie, but his sister wanted him home before Aaron's arrival. It was probably just as well. He had enjoyed his time with Lucy more than he should as a friend.

He guided his buggy onto his property, tied up his horse and hurried toward the house. There wasn't another vehicle in the yard. Relieved that Aaron hadn't arrived yet, he entered through the back, expecting to see Emily bustling about the kitchen as she made the final preparations for supper. Instead his sister sat, elbow on the tabletop, her chin propped up on her hand.

The wonderful aroma of chicken filled the air, and she had set the table for three people, except one place setting had been shoved aside. Emily didn't say a word.

He frowned. Something was seriously wrong. "Em?"

She blinked. "Gabriel." She gazed at him, her eyes dull and filled with unhappiness. "Aaron's not coming."

Her response sparked his anger as he pulled off his hat and hung it on a wooden peg by the door. Covering her hand with his, he sat down beside her. "Why not?"

"I don't know," she said, blinking back tears as she straightened in her chair. "He canceled at the last minute. He didn't tell me why. *He sent his bruder.*" She rose and moved toward the stove. "You must be hungry," she said, her voice flat as she turned on a burner to reheat the meal. "I made fresh bread if you want any and lemon cake for dessert." She faced him, her eyes awash with unshed tears. "I worked hard to make him a meal, and he cancels!" She grabbed bowls off the dining table.

Gabriel gently extracted the dishes from her hands. "Sit, Em. Let me get supper on the table, and then we'll talk, *ja*?"

She sniffed. "I'm not hungry."

"You have to eat, *schweschter*. Are you going to let him keep you from taking care of yourself?" He hesitated. "Maybe he has a *gut* reason why he couldn't come."

Emily plopped onto a chair. "What should I do?" she asked as he took the bowls to the stove.

Gabriel had never seen his sister so upset over a man before. He ladled out chicken potpie then gave her a steaming bowl and kept one for himself. He poured each of them a glass of iced tea and took a seat.

"Try not to judge Aaron, not until you know why he didn't come." He spooned up a taste of the chicken dish. "He may have had a family emergency."

Staring at her supper, she used her spoon to play with her food. "I guess."

Rubbing his chin, he studied her. "You like him, *ja*?"

"Ja." She set her spoon on the table. "But what if he doesn't like me the same way?"

"He agreed to come, didn't he?" He smiled. "You need to trust your feelings. What are they telling you?"

Emily blinked. "You're giving me relationship advice," she said with awe. Suddenly, she narrowed her eyes and stared at him. "You look different, happier. Where were you earlier?"

Gabriel opened his mouth then closed it, unsure what to tell her.

When he didn't immediately answer, she gasped. "You have a sweetheart! You didn't buy the chocolate cream pie!" she exclaimed with surprise. "A woman made it for you!"

"I don't have a sweetheart." His neck burned with discomfort as his sister studied him. "I might have helped a neighbor with a couple of things," he admitted, rubbing a hand across his nape. He sighed. "And *ja*, she made the pie for me as a thank-you for helping her."

Emily looked thoughtful. "The fact that you've spent time with any woman…"

"'Tis nothing," Gabriel said, wondering if it was true. "She's just a neighbor."

"A pretty neighbor?"

He stared at her. "Have you forgotten about Lizzy?"

"Ah, an older one, then."

"Emily, have you forgotten this?" He gestured toward his left leg.

"Gabriel, you deserve to be happy. Lizzy wasn't the right one. Someone else—this woman—might be."

Gabriel didn't comment. He was relieved to see her eat several spoonfuls of her potpie without forcing words from him that he wasn't ready to give. He froze when she stopped eating and met his gaze. He didn't want to talk about Lucy.

"I want to know why Aaron couldn't come," she

said. She worried her bottom lip. "What if he changed his mind about me?"

He relaxed at the change in subject. "I doubt that's the reason. You've been seeing him for what? Almost a month?" She nodded. The man had better have a good explanation why he'd canceled on his sister. Gabriel eyed her thoughtfully. "When will you see him again?"

"We didn't make plans, but I should see him on Sunday. He attends church service faithfully. The change in our friendship is fairly new. No one knows that we have been seeing each other, except for you."

"What about his *bruder*? He must know something."

"I doubt it." Sadness filled her expression. "Nathaniel didn't appear to think anything other than Aaron being invited to a dinner at a neighbor's *haus* he couldn't attend."

Gabriel realized that he had to confide his Sunday plans to her. "Em, I offered to bring a neighbor and her *dochter* to church service. I hope you don't mind riding with them." He fingered the raised scar on his cheek. "I thought I'd stay. It's about time I came back to church."

Emily perked up. "Gabriel, I'm happy you're coming! This isn't Ohio. The people here are different. I like this church community. I've found comfort in the Lord here. I know you will, too. I understand you've been struggling since you got out of the hospital. It's been extremely difficult for you, especially after living with *onkel* Reuben. He made it very clear he didn't want either one of us."

After the house fire that killed his family, when Gabriel had been hospitalized for weeks, Emily had lived with their uncle, their mother's older brother. After he was released, he'd endured living temporarily with

Uncle Reuben, as well. The man, an old bachelor, had considered him and Emily a nuisance. As soon as he was well enough, Gabriel had used the money from the sale of the property that had been their family farm, then he and Emily had moved to New Berne in Lancaster County to make a fresh start.

Here he and his sister had found a measure of peace. Emily had healed from the loss of their family. While his scars remained a constant reminder of the fire, he, too, was on the road to getting over his painful past. The nightmares he'd suffered since the fire came less frequently now. It had been months since his last one. He found himself in a better mood lately, and he thought that might have something to do with meeting and getting to know a certain young widow and her daughter.

Gabriel frowned as he studied Emily, who continued to eat quietly. Aaron Hostetler's absence this evening had upset her. If he found out the man was playing with his sister's affections, he'd have to do something. What, he had no idea.

He dug into his own supper. "This is *wunderbor gut*, Em," he said after swallowing some of her chicken potpie.

She gave him a small smile. "I'm glad you like it. I…" Blinking several times, she stared into her bowl. "I thought I knew him."

"Emily," he said, placing his hand over hers. "Let's see what Aaron has to say first, *ja*?"

She nodded, and her smile became more genuine.

A short time later, they had finished their meal but hadn't enjoyed dessert yet. "Emily, do you mind if I run a quick errand? I'd love a piece of lemon cake when I get back."

His sister gazed at him hard. "You're going to stop by our neighbor's *haus*," she guessed correctly.

He shrugged. "Maybe."

"What's her name?"

"Lucy."

"That doesn't sound like an old neighbor lady's name. Or is that her *dochter*?" she teased with a grin, and he was glad to see her good humor, even if it was at his expense. "Don't be gone too long," she said, "or I'll be forced to eat the whole cake."

Gabriel smiled as he left the house, relieved his sister was fine with him cutting their meal short. He was eager to get back to Lucy. He feared his quick departure earlier had seemed rude to her, and he wanted to make sure she wasn't upset with him.

He was one mile from her house when the pain hit again. Crying out, he steered his buggy to the side of the road to park. The stabbing pain below the skin grafts on his thigh was excruciating. Gasping, he clutched at the limb, rubbing to relieve the agony. His entire leg tensed up. His foot cramped in an extension of his tightening leg muscles, and he breathed harshly, hoping and finally praying that his suffering would stop. Gabriel sat in his buggy for a good while before the sensation started to ease. When it finally left, he was exhausted and discouraged. This second attack this week reminded him that the fire had made him a damaged man.

He waited for a few minutes more until the pain let up. Then, with the memory of his former betrothed Lizzy's claim that he'd never be man enough to take care of her or any woman, Gabriel turned his buggy around and headed home.

* * *

The day after she'd seen Gabriel last, Lucy flipped the last of the pancakes and placed them in a stainless bowl, which she covered with a plate to keep them warm.

"I love pancakes for lunch." Susie sat in her chair, swinging her legs while she waited. "Can I have butter and lots of syrup?"

"Lots of syrup?" Eyeing her daughter, she cracked a smile as she forked two pancakes onto Susie's plate. "You may have syrup, but I'll pour it for you." Susie looked adorable in a bright green tab dress covered with her black apron. She wore her white prayer *kapp* over her blond hair, and her cheeks looked red from excitement and the touch of sun she'd gotten earlier while she'd played in the backyard.

Susie immediately reached for the butter dish, pulling it closer.

"Don't use too much, *dochter*." Lucy watched with satisfaction as her daughter added a small spoonful to her pancakes then spread it around. She poured out Susie's syrup then sank wearily onto her chair. She added a pancake to her plate. She wasn't hungry, though she knew it would be better for the baby if she ate. It had been a while since she'd eaten a decent meal. Her stomach had been bothering her, and since the accident she'd only managed to snack and nibble at her food while Susie ate with gusto.

"Hallo?" The door opened and her sister-in-law stepped in.

Lucy smiled as she stood. She'd expected Nancy to show up earlier in the week after seeing her with Gabriel when she came for Susie. "Want some pancakes? Tea?" she asked.

"Just tea," Nancy said as she approached Susie and rubbed a gentle hand across her niece's shoulder. "How are things?"

"Fine," Lucy said as she poured hot water and fixed tea. "It's been quiet."

"Any visitors?" Nancy asked casually.

Lucy shot her a glance but didn't answer as she carried the tea to the table.

"We saw Gabriel yesterday," Susie piped up, making Lucy inwardly groan.

"Is that right?" Nancy gazed at Lucy with raised eyebrows.

"*Ja*. And on Monday we went out for ice cream after we left your *haus*," her daughter said. "It was *gut*!"

"He's our neighbor," Lucy said. "I had some trouble with my buggy and now it's in the shop."

Her sister-in-law frowned. "What kind of trouble?"

"Something with the axle," she murmured as if she didn't know.

"Gabriel is nice. He took us to the store yesterday, too." She ate the last of her pancakes.

"Susie—"

"He did! And I shared my candy bars with him before he left." Susie grinned at her aunt. "He lives with his sister, and I gave him enough for both of them."

"That was nice of you, Susie," Nancy said, her gaze moving from her niece to Lucy.

"Susie? Why don't you go outside to play? But stay in the backyard, *ja*?"

"*Ja, Mam.*" Susie got up and wiped her mouth with

a napkin. "*Endie* Nancy? Can Sarah and Caleb visit us soon?"

Lucy nodded, and Nancy smiled. "I'm sure we can arrange that."

"*Danki!*" She grabbed her dirty dishes and brought them to the counter next to the sink. Then she ran outside to enjoy the day.

As soon as they were alone, she expected Nancy to question her. Nancy didn't disappoint. "Tell me about Gabriel Fisher."

Lucy shrugged. "He's our neighbor. He lives down the road."

"How did you end up getting a ride from him the other day?"

Lucy shifted uncomfortably. "I had some trouble with my buggy and he stopped to help me. We knew immediately that the buggy needed work done on it. I told him that Susie was at your *haus* and he offered to bring me to get her."

"Hmm," Nancy said noncommittally.

"What?"

"He's a *gut*-looking man despite the scar on his face."

Mention of the scar got Lucy's back up. "You can hardly notice the scar."

"Is there interest between the two of you?" Nancy took a sip of her tea.

"*Nay!*" Lucy exclaimed, her heart beating hard. "He's my neighbor and a nice man."

"That's too bad," her sister-in-law murmured.

Stunned, Lucy blinked. "*What?* Why?"

"You need a man in your life, Lucy."

"*Nay*, I don't. I'm not ready." After Harley, she didn't know if she'd ever be ready.

"You're having a *bubbel*. You need a husband."

"Nancy—"

"If not Gabriel, what about Aaron?"

"*Nay*, not Aaron. I don't feel that way toward him."

"People marry for reasons other than love."

"I won't. Not ever again."

Nancy's expression softened. "I know things were hard on you. Harley wasn't an easy man."

"He still loved Susie's *mudder*."

"You are Susie's *mudder* in every way that counts." Nancy drank the rest of her tea and stood.

"Danki," Lucy whispered as she watched Nancy place their cups in the sink.

"Hallo!" A masculine call came from out in the yard.

Lucy froze. Nancy looked out the window then smirked at her. Lucy opened the door and stepped outside.

"Gabriel!" Susie cried from the backyard. She raced in his direction and gave him a big hug. "I missed you!"

"I missed you, too, little one." His gaze captured and held Lucy's over Susie's head. "I wanted to see you again and to talk with your *mudder*." Her daughter released him, and he smiled at her.

Nancy joined her on the steps. Gabriel saw her and blinked, looking suddenly wary. *"Hallo*, Nancy."

She nodded, crossing her arms and narrowing her gaze at him. "Gabriel."

"Nancy," Lucy whispered warningly. Her sister-in-law grinned at her.

"Come inside, Gabriel," Lucy invited. He entered the house with her and Nancy following.

Susie raced past and climbed onto her chair. Gabriel stood awkwardly in the kitchen.

"Have a seat, Gabriel," Nancy said before facing Lucy. "I've got to get home. I'll see you on Sunday."

"It was nice of you to visit," Lucy said, making Nancy chuckle before she left.

Susie looked from Gabriel to her mother then scrambled from her seat. "*Mam*, I'm going outside again. Gabriel, don't leave without saying goodbye," she told him.

Lucy smiled when she saw him nod. "Be careful and stay in the backyard, *dochter*." She sat down with a tired sigh.

"Are you ill?" Gabriel asked as he studied her closely. He noticed dullness in her normally bright blue eyes. As soon as Lucy's sister-in-law left, he had found himself relaxing, less guarded.

"*Nay*. I'm just tired."

He pulled off his hat and set it on the chair against the wall. His expression filled with concern. "You didn't finish your lunch. You need to eat," he urged softly.

"I know." She stared down at her pancake. "Do you want some pancakes? I'll get you a plate." She started to rise, but Gabriel pushed her gently into her seat.

"*Nay*, I already ate." He watched her until she cut the pancake and took a bite.

"What are you doing here? Do you need something? I just saw you yesterday."

"I just wanted to stop by to see how you're feeling."

"I'm *oll recht*. Well enough to use my wagon to run errands."

He wasn't happy with her driving so soon after the accident. "I thought we talked about this. I don't think you should be handling a horse." He leaned in close to her. "You've still recovering. Your wrist may feel better," he said quietly, "but I bet the rest of you isn't completely healed."

He knew he was right when she grimaced as she shifted in her seat, as if sore. Lucy sighed and put down her fork.

"What's wrong?" He reached across the table to place his hand over hers, enjoying the warmth of it.

"You've done too much already," she said, staring down at their hands. She looked away and he saw her swallow hard.

He gave her left hand a gentle squeeze. "'Tis not a problem."

"You've been kind to us, Gabriel."

"But?" It was difficult for him to resist her. She was his neighbor, but a lovelier woman he'd never met. He was in danger of feeling something more than friendship, but he wouldn't give in to it.

"Are you certain you don't mind taking us to church?" she asked.

"*Ja*, I'm sure." He withdrew his touch as he sat back. He wanted to get back to church although he knew it would be different meeting new people, seeing their reactions to him. Would the congregation stare at his scarred face and make comments? "What time should I come for you Sunday morning?"

"Service is at nine, so eight thirty?"

"I'll be here then." He stood and reached for his hat. "I should get home."

Lucy frowned. "It was kind of you to stop by," she said politely.

Susie entered the house, saw that he held his hat. "Do you have to go?" she asked, her blue eyes filled with sadness.

His eyes grew warm. "I'll see you again soon, little one."

"I wish you didn't have to leave."

He circled the table and touched Susie's cheek. "Be a *gut maydel* for your *mam*."

She grinned up at him. "I will."

Settling his hat on his head, he met Lucy's gaze and remembered the real reason he'd come. He hesitated. "I was wondering… I know 'tis Saturday tomorrow and you probably have a lot to do, but would you and Susie like to go shopping with me?" he asked, hopeful. "At nine thirty? I thought we could look at cell phones."

A little furrow appeared between her eyebrows. "For me?"

Gabriel nodded. "*Ja*. I thought I'd get one, too. For emergency calls, and I think they'll be helpful with our consignment businesses." His smile faded when she didn't immediately give him an answer.

Lucy stared at him as if debating whether or not to go. She finally nodded. "*Ja*, we'll go. I guess having a phone is a *gut* idea."

"*Gut.*" He relaxed. "I'll come for you tomorrow morning at nine."

"*Oll recht.*" Standing on her stoop, he could feel her watching him as he headed toward his buggy.

"Gabriel!" Susie called as she opened the screen door.

Gabriel halted and the child raced to him. She flung herself at him and hugged him about the waist. The movement hurt his leg and he winced before hugging her back. "I wish you didn't have to go," Susie whined.

"I know, little one. I'd like to stay, but I have to get home. But I'll see you tomorrow, *ja*?"

Susie squeezed him again before releasing him and stepping back. He was surprised when Susie tugged on his shirtsleeve, urging his face closer to hers. He bent his head, tilting it as he listened carefully while she whispered in his ear, "I love you, Gabriel."

He felt stunned as he straightened, feeling his whole world light up. He grinned.

As Susie skipped back to her mother, Gabriel captured and held Lucy's gaze. He was surprised to find himself teary-eyed. He had to get out of here before he said something he shouldn't. He doffed his hat, dipped his head and, with a smile, put it on again. Gabriel climbed into his buggy, picked up the leathers and guided his horse onto the road toward home.

As she urged Susie into the house, Lucy wondered what her daughter had said to Gabriel. It looked as if something was bothering Gabriel, but what? He'd looked a little sad until he'd bent down and listened to Susie. She couldn't forget Gabriel's expression after the girl had whispered in his ear.

"What did you tell him?" Lucy asked.

Susie shrugged. "I told him I loved him."

Lucy inhaled sharply. *"Susie,"* she breathed, moved by her amazing, loving child.

"It's true. I love him, *Mam*. I wish I could see him every day."

Gabriel was taking her cell phone shopping, Lucy thought as she washed the breakfast dishes. Maybe they could exchange phone numbers.

By the time Susie was ready to head up to bed that evening, Lucy's wrist ached fiercely. Once Susie was settled, she'd come downstairs and ice it. And try not to think too much about Gabriel Fisher.

The next morning Lucy made potato salad and a chocolate upside-down cake for the meal after Sunday service well before Gabriel was due to arrive at nine. Susie had slept in. When she awoke and found out Gabriel was coming for them, she was excited. Her child loved the man, and Lucy understood why. She should be leery of Gabriel's relationship with Susie, but how could she deny her daughter the influence of a good man? And to see the joy on Gabriel's face was a priceless gift, a blessing from the Lord.

After she stored her homemade potato salad in the refrigerator, she put the cake into a plastic container and set it on the counter. Lucy grabbed her pocketbook and made sure she had her checkbook. She'd opened the account after she'd received the settlement money, and having no idea how much cell phones cost, she figured she'd bring checks just in case.

Susie sat in the great room, looking adorable in a pink tab dress with black apron, white sneakers without socks and her little white prayer *kapp* covering her golden-blond hair. Lucy was back to wearing her dark purple mourning dress but she wore a white apron instead of black. On her feet, she wore sneakers.

It was only eight thirty, and Gabriel wasn't due for another half hour. Lucy was excited to see him again. She knew it was crazy to like someone this much after knowing him such a short time. But how could she forget the way he'd come to the rescue, his calming voice and his inherent ability to make her feel as if everything would be all right? He was a man worth having as a friend. But each time she saw him she liked him more. She'd never expected to be involved with another man, but his kindness and caring made her glad they were friends.

Promptly at nine, she heard the sounds of a buggy through the screen door. Gabriel was right on time. She smiled as Susie ran to open the door.

"Gabriel!" her daughter cried.

Lucy grinned, pleased to see him. She reached the door just as Susie swung it open wide and raced down the steps to meet him. She suffered a moment's fear that her visitor might not be Gabriel, but Susie's cry of happiness quickly put it to rest. She followed in her daughter's footsteps. Gabriel got out of his buggy and smiled, ready for Susie's hug. Her heart leaped as she witnessed the affection between them.

"I'm so glad you came, Gabriel," Susie gushed. "*Mam* said we're going shopping. I'd like to go with you and *Mam*. Do you know where we're going? Do you need to buy something? What is it?"

Her daughter's discourse was nonstop as Lucy approached. Gabriel's gaze captured hers and a warm light flickered in his dark eyes, causing her heart to race and a tingle to start down the entire length of her spine.

"*Hallo*, Gabriel."

She watched him heft Susie into his arms. "*Gut* morning, Lucy. I see you two are ready for our outing."

Susie had put her arms around Gabriel's neck. She removed one to pat him on his right check, the uninjured one. "*Ja*, we are," Lucy murmured as she continued to watch their easy relationship. *I trust him*, she thought, *more than I've ever trusted another man.*

"Susie," she said, looking down at her child's bare feet. "What did you do with your shoes?"

"I took them off," she said.

"Go and get them. You can't go to the store barefoot."

"Ja, Mam." Susie wiggled until Gabriel set her down. While Susie ran inside to get them, Gabriel and Lucy gazed at each other.

"It's nice of you to take us. The more I think about it, the more I realize that having a cell phone is a *gut* idea."

With a small smile reaching his eyes, he nodded. He glanced at her mouth before looking away.

She drew in a sharp breath. "Gab—"

"I got them, *Mam*!" Susie cried, interrupting the tension-filled moment. "Can you help me put them on?"

She dragged her gaze from Gabriel to her daughter. "Sit on the top step, *dochter*, so I can reach better."

Susie kept moving her feet, making it hard for Lucy to tie her shoes.

"Little one," Gabriel said, "stay still so your *mudder* can do your laces."

To Lucy's surprise, her daughter immediately obeyed. Soon they were all in Gabriel's buggy, heading toward the store. Susie sat on the bench between them. "Where are we going?" Lucy asked, curious.

"There's a cell phone place next to King's." He flashed her a smile. "I thought we'd try there."

She nodded, familiar with the store. Her spirits rose as Gabriel seemed more relaxed, happy, the tension between them gone.

He guided his horse into the lot next to a small store that sold cell phones and other items Lucy was unfamiliar with. After maneuvering his buggy to a hitching post, he secured his horse as Lucy climbed out of the vehicle and helped Susie.

He held out his hand to Susie. "Come, little one. Let's see what's inside."

Following behind them, Lucy realized that she was beginning to care a lot for this kind, sensitive man—and she wasn't sure what to do about it.

Chapter Seven

"**Y**ou're going to love this one," the saleswoman said as she held up a cell phone.

Gabriel made himself focus on the phone to keep from staring at the woman helping them. She had short purple hair and a nose ring.

"Look!" The young woman turned the phone on and shifted the screen to where Gabriel and Lucy could see it. "You can surf the net, do email and take photos. There are any number of apps you can download."

Gabriel exchanged a brief, horrified look with Lucy. "That's too fancy for us," he said kindly. "Do you have anything simpler?"

The lady, whose name tag read Bett, stared at him for several long seconds. "You mean like a flip phone?"

"What's a flip phone?" Lucy asked. Her daughter was getting antsy, and Gabriel watched as she calmed Susie with a tender touch to her shoulder.

Shaking her head as if she didn't understand why anyone would want a simple phone, Bett rummaged inside a display case. Within seconds, she straightened, holding a small black-and-white box.

Gabriel watched carefully as she worked to open it. He looked at Lucy and saw amusement curve the corners of her pretty mouth. Susie tugged on her dress hem, drawing her attention. *"Dochter,"* Lucy scolded gently. "Just a little while longer."

He hadn't known Lucy long, yet he found himself wondering what it would be like to have more than friendship with her. She was a sweet and caring woman and an amazing mother. He enjoyed the way she expertly handled her four-year-old daughter. She didn't raise her voice or pull her up by the arm after Susie sat down on the floor when she got tired of waiting.

"You need to be a *gut maydel* for a bit longer. I know you're tired and want to go home, but this shopping is important." She paused, bending to caress Susie's cheek with her fingers.

"We've never owned phones before," Lucy told Bett. "Will they cost a lot?"

The saleswoman stared at her hard then, as realization dawned, her face brightened. "You want a phone with no monthly fees. Ah." She grinned. "You want a burner phone!"

"A burner phone?" Gabriel wasn't sure what that was, but anything with the word *burn* in the name couldn't be good.

Bett chuckled. She grabbed two boxes from beneath the counter after putting the other one away. "I think these might be the ones for you. They're burner flip phones. There is a very small service fee each month that will give you thirty minutes of talk time. If you run out of minutes, you can purchase a card to add more." She showed them what she meant. "And you can buy battery packs that can charge them six or more times.

The packs will be charged after they run out, but you could stop here to do that. Unless you know someone with electricity."

Lucy leaned closer to him. "What do you think?" she whispered.

He gave a little nod while he grinned at her. He was sure that Mary King would allow them to charge their battery packs when they needed to. Gabriel turned to Bett. "We'll take two of the burner phones." He gestured toward the boxes. "We'll get the phones and two battery packs. I'll help whenever you need it," he added to Lucy.

She gave him a soft smile, and he felt his heart thump hard.

"Mam?" Susie tugged on her mother's dress hem. "Are we almost done?"

"Ja, dochter, we're almost done," she said, holding his gaze.

He grinned at her. While Lucy was busy with Susie, Gabriel completed the transaction and paid for a year's service fees in advance. He asked Bett to put his phone number in Lucy's phone and his in hers.

"I'll put you both on speed dial. You'll only have to press a two on your phone to call each other."

Minutes later, they left the store with Gabriel carrying the bag with everything. "Now, where would you like to go to lunch?" he asked, and Susie cried out with joy.

"Can we eat ice cream?"

"Susie Schwartz!" Lucy scolded. "What did I tell you about asking for treats?"

The little girl gazed at her mother with a look of innocence. "I didn't ask for candy, *Mam.*"

Gabriel had to stifle a chuckle. "*Mam*, she has a point there," he whispered in her ear when Susie couldn't hear.

Lucy slid him an irritated sideways look. "Don't encourage her, Gabriel Fisher."

"I wouldn't do something like that," he said, but his huge grin said otherwise. "Well? What are you hungry for?"

"It's too early to eat," she said. "I should get home."

"Mam!" Susie whined but she stopped immediately after one stern look from her mother.

"Susie," Lucy said firmly, "'Tis time to go home."

Gabriel was disappointed that he wouldn't get to spend more time with her. "Come on, then, and I'll take you back."

Lucy gazed at him with a furrowed brow. "I'm sorry, but I have things to do," she said. "Tomorrow is Sunday." She was silent as he lifted Susie onto the buggy seat.

When he faced her, he saw worry in her expression, and he knew it was because her buggy would be in the shop for some time.

"Gabriel…" She sighed.

"I understand, Lucy. Besides, I'll be picking you up for service tomorrow morning, *ja*?"

She looked relieved. "You really don't mind?"

"Not at all." He felt encouraged that he hadn't suffered another episode of leg pain since the other evening. If he stayed careful, it was possible it wouldn't happen again. And it gave him hope. The realization that he'd be seeing Lucy again soon was enough to lighten his spirits, even if it was just taking her to church service tomorrow morning.

He helped her into his buggy and a short time later

pulled up close to her door. He carefully climbed down and hurried to the other side to help Lucy and her daughter out.

"Here's your phone," he told her as he handed Lucy a box. "Bett put our numbers on speed dial. We just have to hit the number two to call each other." He patted Susie's head. She had pulled off her prayer *kapp* during the trip home. "Be *gut* and I'll see you both in the morning."

"How much do I owe you?" Lucy asked.

Gabriel named the cost minus the battery pack. He could buy his friend a battery pack if he wanted, couldn't he? "I paid for a year's service, too. You can pay me later." He turned to leave then stopped to look back, watching as Lucy unlocked her door and entered the house with Susie.

When the door closed behind them, Gabriel climbed back into his buggy. As he rode down the lane, he tried not to think about church service in his new community. The devastating loss of his family after the fire and his lengthy recovery from his burns plus the complications had made it impossible for him to attend service back in his Amish community in Ohio.

And if truth be known, he'd been more than a little angry at what had happened. By the time he'd moved here, his anger had dissipated enough to make him realize that the fire wasn't anyone's fault. Things happened in life that challenged people, and he needed to face his challenges and do what was right. Then Lucy had entered his life and made a huge impact. God had given another sign that it was the right time for him to attend church service again and be grateful that while he couldn't save his other family members, he'd been able to get Emily out not only alive but unharmed. And he was blessed to now have Lucy and her daughter in his life.

While he felt ready to go back to church, it didn't mean he wasn't nervous. He'd never gotten used to people staring because of his facial scar. But because of Lucy—and Susie—he was beginning to feel better about his situation. As long as his leg didn't continue to be a problem, Gabriel could allow himself small hope that he might be able to have a life where he didn't focus on the failures of being unable to save his parents, two brothers and his youngest sister. Could he have a future filled with love, something he hadn't trusted or believed in since Lizzy had abandoned him? The flare-ups in his leg seemed constant reminders that he'd basically become disabled after the fire.

Lizzy would have made a terrible wife, he realized when he thought back to their relationship. Any woman who could abandon her future husband in his time of need clearly hadn't loved him to begin with.

Gabriel never thought he'd find joy in living again. But his new friendship with Lucy made him feel good. He enjoyed spending time with her. He was glad he'd been the one to help her after her accident. Something had shifted inside of him when she'd looked to him for support. It was as if the Lord was reminding him that there were wonderful things worth living for.

Like Susie. What a precious little girl! Lucy's daughter had taken one look at him and immediately accepted him. He couldn't remember the last time he'd felt that comfortable with anyone other than his sister.

And Lucy? His heart leaped. She accepted him, too. If he wasn't a broken man and Lucy hadn't lost her husband recently, he might have had a chance with her. God had given him Lucy as a friend, and he would treasure and keep the relationship safe. As he drove closer to home, Gabriel prayed that nothing would ever ruin their friendship.

Sunday morning dawned bright and clear. Dressed in their Sunday best, Lucy and Susie waited for Gabriel on the front porch. It was a lovely spring morning. Birds chirped, filling the air with their beautiful song. Sunlight on the grass made the lawn look greener. A soft breeze rustled the leaves in the trees and slipped under the porch roof, bringing with it the scent of the flowers she'd planted along one side of the porch.

Unbidden came thoughts of her late husband. For the most part, their marriage was as she'd expected it to be between two strangers marrying for convenience and the love of a child. Harley had been quiet at first, grieving for his dead wife. Lucy had understood. She was grieving in her own way for the loss of her mother— and the loving man she'd mistakenly thought her father was while *Mam* was alive.

She and Harley had settled into married life. He hadn't been unkind but he'd kept himself distant from her. She'd taken care of Susie and kept house while Harley had worked and done all the things that men were supposed to do. By the second year, Harley had been friendlier. He'd begun to smile more often, and Lucy had felt content with her marriage and life. If Harley got in a bad mood every once in a while, Lucy didn't let it bother her. She'd figured he would get out of it on his own time.

Now, with Harley gone, Lucy wasn't afraid to be

alone, but it was nice to know that she had a new friend in Gabriel. The buggy accident had made her realize that life could be frightening, but if she continued to pray and trust in God, she would be fine. For it was God who had sent Gabriel to help her when she most needed someone she could trust.

Her father's selfishness had hurt her deeply. Lucy knew that marriage arrangements happened within Amish communities. But for her father to arrange her marriage because he wanted to get rid of her so that he could take a young wife? And then not have any contact with her after she and Harley moved to New Berne?

Her father's lack of love and warmth was devastating to her. She prayed daily to ask for God's help in forgiving the man who'd sired her. It had been a struggle but she'd finally forgiven her father.

Lucy shoved thoughts of her father from her mind and sought peace instead as she rocked in a white wooden rocking chair on the porch. She had a lot to be grateful for and she would continue to focus on her blessings.

Susie sat next to her in the other chair, looking tiny in the adult-sized seat, her feet swinging above the porch floor.

"Is Gabriel still coming for us?" Susie jerked her body backward hard against the shoulder rest of the chair, throwing her feet up and then down in an effort to move it.

"*Ja*, he'll be here." Smiling at her daughter, she shook her head. "Susie, come and sit with me. I'll rock the chair for you."

"I can do it, *Mam*," she insisted firmly.

"I'm sure you can, but let's sit together for a while, *ja*?" Lucy patted her lap. "I'd like to hug my *dochter*."

Susie grinned and bent forward, tipping the chair until her feet touched the porch floor. She got down from her chair and climbed onto her mother's lap. "I like my Sunday-best dress, *Mam*," her daughter murmured. "We look the same. You wore your blue dress today, just like mine. And you put on a black apron, too."

Her daughter settled herself onto Lucy's lap and stretched out her legs to peer at her shoes. Like many others in the community, Susie often went barefoot during the warmer months, but on church Sundays she wore her black stockings and shoes. Lucy wore a royal blue dress like her daughter's, and each wore matching white organza, heart-shaped head coverings, familiar and identifiable to Lancaster County, Pennsylvania.

Lucy enjoyed wearing something other than her drab purple mourning dress she'd worn for over five months now and was more than ready to give up for good. She didn't think anyone would say a word about her dress today. Even Nancy had been telling her that she should think about marrying again. And she would eventually. She smiled as she recalled the group of women who'd come to visit, widows who'd remarried and now enjoyed a happier life. Life was too short not to live it to the fullest, she decided. Maybe Rachel and Hannah were right and she shouldn't dismiss the idea of finding a new life with a man she could love.

Gabriel's image came to mind…his smile, the warmth in his brown eyes, the kindness and compassion in his expression. Since meeting Gabriel, with his good humor and affection for Susie, she wondered if he could possibly be the man she could build a life with—if, over time, their friendship could turn into something more.

A buggy entered the yard and drove toward the house, drawing her attention.

"Gabriel!" Susie cried as she sprang from Lucy's lap. "We're over here!"

As if he'd heard her cry, he rolled up to the front porch rather than the side door where he often parked. Lucy rose to her feet slowly as he climbed out of his vehicle and approached. She smiled at him as he drew near. "*Gut* morning, Lucy. Susie," he greeted each of them with a nod.

"Are you ready to go, Gabriel?" Susie asked sweetly.

His smile for Susie was soft. "*Ja*, little one." Gabriel searched for Lucy, finding and holding her gaze over Susie's head, his expression warm as he watched her closely.

"*Mam*, don't forget the cake!" Susie cried as she ran down the porch steps and rushed to give Gabriel a hug. He lifted her into the back seat then waited to help Lucy into the front. Minutes later, they were on their way, Gabriel turning onto the street.

Lucy faced front, gazing at the pavement through the buggy's windshield.

"You look *nice* in your Sunday best dress, Lucy," he said, drawing her attention.

Feeling flustered, she blushed, unsure what to say. She averted her gaze, looking through the side window. "I appreciate the ride, Gabriel."

"You are *willkomm*, Lucy."

She saw amusement in his eyes when she looked at him again. Embarrassed, she stared ahead and realized they were going the wrong way. "Gabriel, this isn't the way to the Troyers."

"I know, but my sister wasn't ready, and I promised to go back for her."

He pulled onto the driveway to his house. A pretty woman with red hair and green eyes waited for him. He got out to help her in.

She waited patiently as Emily climbed into the back with Susie, carrying a plastic container. *"Hallo,"* she said to her little girl.

"Hallo," Susie said cautiously. "Gabriel? Who is this?"

Emily laughed. "He isn't *gut* with introductions. I'm Emily, and Gabriel is my *bruder.*" She shifted to the middle of the seat, closer to Lucy's daughter, and tapped Lucy on the shoulder. "Lucy, right? Our neighbor and Gabe's friend?"

"Ja, and the little one next to you is Susie, my *dochter."* Lucy felt more than a little relieved. Turning sideways to better see Emily and Susie, she flashed Gabriel's sister a genuine smile. "Nice to meet you, Emily."

The woman's expression warmed. "Same here." She leaned back in her seat. "What have you got in the dishes, Susie?"

"Chocolate cake and potato salad." Susie tilted her head thoughtfully as she looked at the plastic container in Emily's hands. "What are those?"

"Lemon squares."

"I love lemon squares," Susie said, her eyes lighting up.

"My *dochter* loves sweets," Lucy said.

Emily chuckled as she jerked a nod at her brother's head. "She's not the only one."

Lucy was amused to see red rise to Gabriel's cheeks. She'd have to remember that and make sure she made him baked goods often. He never did say whether or not he'd enjoyed the pie she'd given him.

As Susie and Emily chatted in the back, Lucy and Gabriel rode quietly in the front as he drove them to Sunday service. He looked over and met her gaze. They exchanged smiles, but she saw something in his expression that told her he was nervous. Without thought, she touched his arm briefly to comfort him. When he looked at her with surprise, she felt the sudden, strong awareness between them.

Heart racing, Lucy quickly looked away. Her attention didn't leave the road until he guided his horse onto the Troyer property and parked his buggy at the end of a long row of gray family vehicles parked side by side. Only then did she look in Gabriel's direction. Their gazes locked for several seconds before he broke away to get out and tie up his horse, then he reached in to help Susie from the back. Lucy scrambled down on her own and collected her food offerings from the back while Gabriel gently lifted his sister down.

Lucy didn't know what to think as they headed toward the yard, where church members chatted while waiting for service to begin. She saw Aaron across the lawn, talking with three older men. He glanced and nodded in her direction. She gave him the briefest nod and joined the group of young women who had visited her recently. Hannah and Rachel grinned as they spied her.

"Mam," Susie said with a tug on her shirtsleeve. "Can I go over and see Sarah and Caleb?"

Her attention followed Susie's to where her sister-in-law stood with a group of women on the side lawn.

"You may say a quick *hallo*, but then come right back. Service will be starting soon."

With a bob of her head, Susie ran to her cousins.

She glanced back, saw Gabriel and Emily near the house, waiting for service. Pulled by emotion, Lucy headed in their direction. When her daughter joined them moments later, she felt complete.

Sensing someone's stare, she glanced back to see Nancy. Her sister-in-law looked in Gabriel's direction with raised eyebrows.

Lucy felt her face heat. Her world seemed to spin in all directions whenever she was in Gabriel's company.

Chapter Eight

Service was about to start. Lucy and Susie sat in the women's section with Hannah Brubaker, Rachel King and their girls in front of them. Gabriel's sister Emily sat next to her with Nancy and Sarah behind her. Gabriel was near the back of the men's area, looking uncomfortable, and Lucy wished she could reassure him somehow that he was welcome within their community.

Maggie Troyer's husband, Thomas, church deacon, entered the preaching area and welcomed everyone to service. It opened with a song from the *Ausbund*, the Amish book of hymns. After that, everyone turned to "Das Loblied," "Hymn of Praise"—the second hymn always chosen for church service. The singing went on for a half hour or more before the preacher, David Bontrager, rose to speak.

Susie was good during service. Attending regularly since she was a baby, she was used to behaving—and being reverent—during worship. Lucy stole frequent glances toward Gabriel and was glad to see him join in the hymns and listen carefully to the preacher. At one point, Gabriel's gaze locked with hers, and Lucy felt her face redden before she hastily looked away.

Service lasted three hours, then everyone stood to get ready for the community meal that followed. The men immediately went to work moving the church benches outside to use as seats. The tables were made of plywood over sawhorses. Capturing Susie's hand, Lucy took her into Maggie's kitchen where the churchwomen collected and carried the food outside. Their church district was actually small compared to others.

Rachel King smiled at them. "I'm glad to see that you're staying. We're eating outside today since it's sunny and *warum*." The woman picked up two plates of cold meat and carried them out into the yard.

The hostess, Maggie, leaned into the refrigerator to pull out food containers, which she set on the counter. "What can we do to help?" Lucy asked her.

Maggie held Lucy's bowl of potato salad. "Would you take this outside?" She smiled. "Susie, would you carry out the paper plates and napkins?"

Susie bobbed her head and was handed a package each of paper plates and napkins. "When you come back, I'll give you something else to carry," Maggie said.

Lucy followed her daughter outside. "Just put them on the first table," she told her daughter. She carried her salad to the table and found a place for it. "Let's go back inside and see what else we can help with."

Minutes later, she watched Susie carry a box of forks toward a table. Gabriel approached Susie and, smiling gently, he helped her find the right spot for the forks.

Her heart melted when she saw Gabriel's soft expression as her daughter walked to the house. He was quickly winning her over with his kindness and caring concern for Susie and her.

Her daughter ran to the group of children in the backyard. Lucy could hear their laughter through the window screen.

"Susie is growing up too quickly," a feminine voice said from behind her.

Lucy turned and saw Rachel King, who must have been watching her daughter. "*Ja*, she is." She sighed. "Hard to believe she'll be five soon. It seems like yesterday when she was a tiny *bubbel*."

"Susie needs a father," Rachel said. "Maybe Aaron?"

"*Nay*," Lucy answered quickly. "I don't think of Aaron in that way." Her gaze sought and settled on Gabriel Fisher, who was now chatting with Jed King.

"Lucy, who is that with my Jed?"

Lucy blinked and felt heat rise to her cheeks. "That's Gabriel Fisher. He and his sister Emily are my neighbors. They gave me and Susie a ride this morning."

Rachel studied Gabriel with the intensity of someone who wanted to learn more about him, before she met Lucy's gaze. "He is a *gut*-looking man even with that scar."

"*Ja*, he is," Lucy agreed, slightly upset that Rachel had mentioned it until she realized that her friend had never met Gabriel before today.

"Maybe a better man than Aaron?"

She averted her gaze. "I don't know him that well."

"But you'd like to," Rachel said, drawing Lucy's glance. There was a spark in the woman's eyes that made her uneasy. Maybe because Lucy did find Gabriel attractive.

"I should check on Susie," Lucy said, wanting only

to escape. She slipped outside into the yard and watched as her *dochter* ran back to Gabriel. Susie stopped and grinned up at him, her little arms reaching out to him. Gabriel looked happy to have her near.

Emotion tightened Lucy's throat until she could barely swallow past the painful lump—something akin to love intermingled with joy, satisfaction…and hope. They were on the far side of the lawn. Lucy started in their direction when a hand on her arm stopped her. She halted and glanced back to see Aaron Hostetler, his expression earnest and caring.

"Aaron!"

"We need to talk, Lucy." Aaron glanced past her and frowned, then quickly pulled her toward a shade tree.

"Why?" she asked, resisting his touch. "What do you want?"

"I worry about you," he said, his voice thick.

She softened her expression. "I know you do, but I'm fine. You need to stop worrying about me and live your life."

"Lucy, what if I want to make you my life? What if I want to marry you?"

She gaped at him with horror. "*Nay*, you don't want that. *I* don't want that." She made it several steps before he caught her arm.

"*Please.* Let me talk to you for a minute."

Lucy sighed. "What is it?"

"I feel responsible for you."

She frowned. "Why?"

"Because if it wasn't for me, Harley would be alive!" he whispered urgently.

"What are you talking about?" Lucy stared at him. "He died in a truck accident."

"Harley wasn't supposed to be in that truck—I was."

Lucy's expression softened. "You didn't send him to his death, Aaron. He died because it was his time."

"But that's not all." Aaron looked miserable. "That night he came home after drinking? I brought him home."

"I'm glad you did—"

"*Nay!* I brought him home and I should have gone inside to make sure he was *oll recht*, that *you* were *oll recht*."

"Aaron, there was no reason for you to come inside that night. Harley was fine. He fell asleep in a chair."

"But not before—" His gaze settled on her arm, and she knew that he was referring to the slight mishap with a knife when her husband had been a bit vigorous trying to get her attention while she'd been making supper.

"Is that what this is all about?" she asked him. "You feel responsible for that?"

Aaron's blue eyes held sadness and remorse. "Lucy—"

She sighed heavily. "Aaron, you had nothing to do with my little injury or my late husband's death." She softened her expression. "*Gott* has a plan for each of us, and what happened was part of it. Now go and find yourself a sweetheart. You deserve to have your own life—not become part of mine because of something you had no control over."

His expression brightened with hope. "You really feel this way?"

Lucy grinned. "I do."

Aaron gave a jerk of his head as if he finally understood and walked away with a small smile.

Feeling much better, Lucy planned to enjoy the

shared meal. She looked for Susie and found her eating with Sarah and Caleb. She filled a plate and looked around to see if Gabriel and Emily wanted to join them, but they were already seated with Mary and James King. The bishop and church elders often allowed families to eat together when the meal was shared outside, forgoing the normal practice of the men sitting down to eat first and the women and children eating after the men were done.

Lucy smiled, glad that Gabriel was feeling comfortable enough to join other community members. She took a seat at the table next to Nancy while Susie and Sarah sat on Nancy's opposite side. Nancy's husband, Joseph, and Caleb sat across from them.

"*Mam*, I'm going to eat my meat and vegetables before I have dessert," Susie said.

"I told her it's the best way to stay healthy and get big," eight-year-old Caleb interjected before Lucy could say a word.

"*Ja*, that's *gut* advice, Caleb. Susie, I'm glad to see you eating like you should."

Susie nodded before she ate another bite-size piece of cold roast beef. "*Mam*, where's Gabriel?"

"He's eating with the Kings."

"How come he didn't want to eat with us?" her daughter asked with a frown.

"*Dochter*, Gabriel is making new friends. That's *gut*, *ja*?"

"*Ja*, as long as he doesn't forget us."

Gazing at her softly, Lucy rubbed a hand over Susie's shoulder. "He won't forget us."

"*Nay*, he won't forget you," Nancy agreed with a smirk.

A half hour later, Lucy felt sick. She didn't know if it had to do with her pregnancy or something she ate. "I think I need to go home and lie down," she told Nancy as she stood. Susie had run off to play with her cousins and other children. Judging from the shrieks and wild laughter, they were all having a great time.

"Do you want us to take you home?" Joseph asked, having overheard.

Swallowing against bile, Lucy shook her head. "*Nay,* I came with Gabriel. I'll ask if he'll take me. Will you take Susie home if she wants to stay?"

"*Ja,* of course we will," Nancy said, her gaze filled with concern.

Lucy saw him in a gathering of men talking near the barn. He broke away from the group when he saw her approach.

"Gabriel," she said, hands resting on her belly as she reached his side. "Do you know what time you want to go?"

He frowned as he gazed at her. "You're not feeling well."

She nodded.

He eyed her thoughtfully with concern in his expression. "I'll tell Emily that we're leaving."

Lucy hugged herself with her arms. "Your sister shouldn't have to leave."

His gaze softened. "I wasn't going to ask her to," he assured her. "I'll come back for her later."

Lucy breathed a sigh of relief as Gabriel reached his sister's side. Searching for her daughter, she saw that Susie had stopped playing and was now seated with her cousin on a bench close to the food table. Both girls were eating a piece of her chocolate cake. She hurried over and pulled Susie aside.

"I'm going home to rest, little one. Do you want to come? If not, *Endie* Nancy and *Onkel* Joseph will bring you home later."

Susie frowned. "I can stay?"

"*Ja*, you can stay. Run and tell *Endie* Nancy that you want to stay and play." Lucy smiled as she watched her daughter run off.

"I'll watch out for her," Sarah said, rising as if to follow Susie.

Lucy managed a smile, despite the roiling sensation of being sick to her stomach. "I know you will."

A few minutes later, she waited for Gabriel near the Troyers' barn where families had parked their gray buggies side by side in a long row. Gabriel's was on the farthest side from the house.

Gabriel headed her way, and Lucy felt an overwhelming sense of relief. Aaron stood in the yard, chatting with another group of young men.

A wave of nausea hit her, and she swallowed hard and cradled her abdomen. And prayed she wouldn't get sick before she reached home.

"Lucy?" Gabriel's voice was now soft, filled with concern, and she blinked back tears as he held her gaze.

"I'm *oll recht*." Although she wasn't.

Gabriel studied her for several seconds. "Do you need to get anything from inside the *haus*?" he asked gently.

Lucy shook her head. As the movement settled in, she started to tremble. "Come. Let's get you home."

There was silence in the buggy during the ride. Lucy stared out the side window at the passing scenery, eventually becoming aware of Gabriel's frequent worried looks in her direction.

When they reached the house, he hurried to help her out of his vehicle. Averting her gaze, Lucy thanked him for the ride and started toward the house, unaware that he followed her until she opened her screen door and her hands shook so badly that she nearly dropped her house key. He gently took the key from her and unlocked the door, holding it open for her. Lucy turned to thank him again, but he shook his head while gently urging her inside, following her in.

"Gabriel," she whispered.

He smiled at her with a tenderness she'd never seen from a man before. "I won't stay long. Lucy, sit down before you fall." He pulled out a chair for her. "I know you need to rest, but I'd like to make you a cup of tea before I leave."

Lucy felt in no shape to argue, and maybe the tea would help to settle her queasy stomach. "I wouldn't mind a cup," she finally said.

His slow smile before he turned to grab the kettle from the stove made her neck tingle and her face warm. He filled the teakettle with tap water and set it on a hot burner.

She closed her eyes, breathing deeply and praying that she wouldn't get sick in front of Gabriel.

The teakettle whistled, startling her. She shot a look toward the stove and watched as Gabriel made her a cup of tea. "Black with sugar?" he asked, drawing her attention to his handsome features.

She shivered under the focus of his watchful brown eyes. *"Ja. Danki."* She felt slightly better.

Gabriel stirred in the right amount of sugar, and Lucy

realized with surprise that he'd paid close attention to how she drank it.

"Would a cracker help to settle your stomach?" he asked.

She shook her head. "I don't think I should eat anything right now."

He watched her take a sip of tea. "Is there anything else I can do?"

"*Nay.* This is *gut.*"

He seemed hesitant to leave, but her nausea was returning.

She swallowed hard. "Gabriel."

She saw his eyes widen with understanding. He opened two cabinets before he found a large bowl that he set close to her just in the nick of time. She was sick several times while Gabriel gently kept her *kapp* strings out of the way. She was humiliated, knowing she would no doubt see horror and disgust on the man's face.

She leaned back with her eyes closed, feeling a little better. She braced herself to face him, but before she did, she felt a dry paper towel dab across her mouth before a damp cloth settled on her forehead, and he wiped every part of her face with it. Lucy opened her eyes and saw Gabriel, a man who cared enough to stay and take care of her, someone who didn't seem put off by her getting sick. He went to pick up the dirty bowl.

"*Nay!*" she gasped and lay her hand on top of his.

He froze and locked gazes with her. The feel of his warm hand beneath her fingers felt too good. It seemed in that moment that they might be more than friends. Until he released the bowl and stepped back. Then she felt so embarrassed. How would she ever look at him again without remembering this? She didn't want him to clean up after her. The thought mortified her.

With a silent nod, he headed toward the door. "Take care and rest."

"*Danki*, Gabriel," she said as she got up to follow him. She stood at the door and watched as he climbed into his vehicle and left. Lucy turned back to the table to drink her tea, her thoughts filled with Gabriel Fisher and his kindness and her growing feelings for him. As she sipped her tea, Lucy thought about what it could be like for someone like Gabriel to love her and be a permanent part of her life.

Gabriel guided his horse back to the Troyer house to pick up Emily. He felt bad for Lucy. He knew she was embarrassed, but she had no reason to be. He was actually glad that he could help her.

He saw Emily waiting near the barn for him as he pulled onto the property. He frowned at her unhappy expression. He pulled up close to her and started to get out to help, but she was already climbing into the front seat. "What's wrong, Em?"

His sister took a deep breath then released it. "I spoke with Aaron."

"And?" Waiting patiently for her to answer, he steered the buggy back toward the road.

Emily didn't respond immediately. "I know why Aaron didn't come to supper."

Gabriel frowned. "Why?"

She blinked back tears. "Lucy Schwartz."

"*What?* How do you know?" He didn't like the sinking feeling that settled in his stomach.

"I saw them talking together earlier, so I asked him

about her. And you know what he said?" She closed her eyes and breathed deeply. "That her late husband was his best friend and she is important to him," she burst out.

He saw her rapidly blinking back tears. "Emily, if her husband was his best friend, then she would be important to him." But just how important? Gabriel wondered. Had Aaron been the one he'd seen leaving Lucy's driveway the other day? How close were Aaron and Lucy? His stomach burned at the thought that they might be closer than friends. "So he didn't come to supper because of Lucy?"

"*Nay*, not exactly," she admitted. "I didn't get to ask him about that. I saw him with her this at service, and I had to know what she meant to him."

"And you're upset by what he told you." Gabriel decided he wouldn't get upset until after he'd spoken with Lucy. Then he remembered that they were only friends, and he had no right to be upset. And yet, he cared for her as more than a friend. And that wasn't good. Maybe he should avoid her for a while until he could think things through. If only he could make himself stay away from her…

Chapter Nine

Gabriel sat on the exam table in his neurologist's office in a hospital gown and looked up as the doctor entered the room.

"Gabriel," Dr. Jorgensen greeted him. "Since you're here, I'm guessing that your leg is bothering you."

"Yes," Gabriel said. "Twice in the last week, I had stabbing pains in my thigh. I haven't had any like those in months."

"Let's take a look at your leg." The doctor examined it, pressing several areas of the grafted and scarred skin. "Does this hurt?" He probed a little more, asking questions with every area he touched. When he was done, he sat down on a stool and typed into a computer. He turned to face Gabriel. "I'd like to run a blood test to make sure there is nothing else going on. I don't think there is, but we have to make certain. Let's talk about your options. Have you tried ibuprofen?"

"It doesn't usually work," Gabriel admitted.

"It may if taken regularly. You should take ibuprofen or naproxen. I'll write down the dosage of both, but only take one kind as they are both NSAIDs. I could prescribe some patches for you to try, but the ones over-the-counter work well and are less expensive. Try those with the NSAIDs and we'll see how you do." He turned back to his computer, added entries then faced him again. "There are a number of other things we can do if you continue to experience this type of neuropathic nerve pain without relief."

"Will it ever go away?" Gabriel asked. "The pins and needles? The stabbing pains?"

Dr. Jorgensen, a gray-haired man with green eyes that were filled with compassion right now, gazed at him for a long moment. "It's hard to say. I can't tell you for sure. It's possible, but it's also possible that your pain may be chronic."

Gabriel felt his chest tighten. "So I have to learn to live with it."

"It's possible. Only time will tell. I can say that sometimes it just takes a little longer for nerves to heal. You suffered burns severe enough to require skin grafts, and from your records, I know you had problems with infection with the burns and after your first skin grafting that required you to undergo more surgery." The man stood, offering a reassuring smile. "Try not to worry. I'll help you manage your pain so that you can enjoy your life. And with time you may find that you no longer feel any pain, except for the occasional paresthesia—the pins and needles sensation. Even that could go away." He smiled and walked Gabriel to the front desk to check out. "I'd like to see you back in two weeks for a follow-up." He wrote on a pad, ripped off the sheet of paper and gave it to him. "Instructions for the NSAID and patches." He studied Gabriel thoughtfully. "Have you had physical therapy?"

"After my surgery."

"It's something else to consider if your pains continue. There are other methods we can try to manage your pain. If your pain worsens after we've exhausted all other avenues, we may want to consider surgery as a last resort."

Gabriel nodded. He didn't ask more about what surgery could do for him. He didn't want to be operated on. Although he wasn't sure physical therapy would work, he was willing to give it a try first. He'd try anything to stop his leg from hurting except surgery. The thought of another hospital stay and weeks if not months of recovery chilled him to the bone. He'd spent too much time in the hospital recovering from his burns and skin-graft surgeries to forget the horrible experience.

Minutes later, he left his doctor's office and headed for home, stopping once along the way to pick up naproxen and the pain patches his doctor wanted him to use. He hoped they worked. If not, he would have to try something else.

Chronic pain. That wasn't what he wanted to hear. But he wouldn't give up hope. Pins and needles he could live with. That sensation could be uncomfortable at times, but it was the stabbing pain that stole his breath and made it nearly impossible for him to walk that he feared most. He hoped it wouldn't become chronic. He had things to do and a life to lead.

An image of Lucy came to mind, and he had to wonder why it suddenly seemed important that he get better fast. For her. Until he remembered Aaron Hostetler. He needed to ask Lucy about the man.

The following morning bright and early Gabriel sat on his stool at his workbench and carefully eyed the piece of basswood he held. He was finally going to make the toy for Susie. If he was going to ask Lucy about Aaron, he needed another reason to go over as well, and he planned on gifting Susie the toy. The duck toy would be made from three types of wood: birch, pine and basswood. Using a carpenter's pencil, he sketched out the head, body and legs and used a handheld coping saw to cut out each part. He then sanded the edges smooth before he assembled them together.

An hour after he'd started, he was done with the toy except for the finish. He tested it, watching as the wooden duck easily waddled down the elevated wooden track. He smiled as he envisioned the child who would be playing with it. He brushed on a clear coat of varnish and set it aside to dry.

He left the workshop then and headed toward the barn area he'd decided could be sectioned off and renovated for his wooden crafts store. Sunday after they'd gotten home, he'd brought Emily into the barn and told her of his plans, hoping to distract her from Aaron. He'd asked if she would help him by working in the store with him once it was ready.

Emily had smiled at him. "You're going to do it!"

"'Tis time, don't you think?"

"*Ja*, and it will be *wunderbor*."

"What are you going to call it?" she'd asked with a thoughtful smile. "Your store?"

"I don't know. I haven't given it any thought."

"I'll think of a few names and you can choose."

Now Gabriel studied the space that needed to be renovated. His first order of business was to section off an area with the addition of a new wall and an entrance door. After that, he'd cover the walls with Sheetrock and layer over the concrete floor with linoleum. He would need a sales counter where they would wait on customers. He could do the work himself, but not without suffering afterward. Which meant he had to find someone who worked in construction.

Still, Gabriel was excited. Having his own store would be worth the extra cost. He wouldn't have to make early morning deliveries anymore, nor would he have to share his profits with another store owner.

He smiled as he envisioned how the store would look after the work was done. He had no idea why but he had the sudden urge to tell Lucy about his plans. It was Tuesday, and he hadn't seen her since Sunday afternoon when he'd brought her home. He wondered how she was doing. Thoughts of her brought with them thoughts of Aaron Hostetler, and he didn't want to think about the two of them together.

Forcing his thoughts back to his store, Gabriel decided to ask Jed King, who worked with his parents at King's General Store, whom he should hire. He'd recently learned that Jed had previously worked in construction.

He went back to his workshop where he'd left his cell phone. After a quick check on the drying status of Susie's waddling duck toy, he made the call to Jed King.

Seated at the kitchen table, Lucy wrote a check for the repairs to her buggy. It was late morning Tuesday, two days after church day and the last time she'd seen Gabriel, and she still felt embarrassed that she'd gotten sick in front of him. Rachel King had stopped by an hour ago with a message that had been left by Lapp's Carriage Shop at the general store for her. Eli Lapp had fixed her buggy and the vehicle was ready to be picked up. Staring at the check, she cringed at the amount that would be taken from her bank balance. It was a large chunk of the settlement check from her late husband's employer. Thankfully, though, her baked items had sold well at King's and Peter's Pockets.

She still owed Gabriel for the cell phone and accessories—and that wasn't all she owed him. She knew why he was staying away. No one wanted to see their friend get sick, although Gabriel had been sweet about it. She knew she should call him or go over to his house to pay him, but she was still too humiliated.

She missed him, she realized. Lucy wondered when she would see him again. *If* she'd see him again. Even Susie had asked when Gabriel was going to visit them.

At least Lucy was feeling much better than she had been on Sunday afternoon.

The windows were open to allow fresh air to filter in throughout the house. Susie sat on the floor with crayons and paper. Her daughter had already drawn several pictures, which Lucy had placed on the refrigerator with magnets.

It didn't matter what her little girl was doing, Susie always made her feel better. Lucy would have been content to watch Susie all day, but she needed to get baking. Mary King and John Zook both needed more cakes and other bakery items from her. She hoped to expand her business to other stores, and Gabriel had offered to help with that, but they'd never actually discussed it. The next time she saw him, she'd have to ask.

She liked the idea of opening her own bakery, except she didn't want to spend the cash needed to rent a storefront right now. Besides, once her baby was born in two months, there'd be no time to run her own bakery. Maybe she'd open one after her children were old enough to be on their own. It was more important to be there for Susie and her baby, so selling on consignment was the best way for her to make a living right now.

She felt a flutter of life inside her as her baby moved, something her child was doing more and more each day. Lucy stood, her hand on her pregnant belly. She was nearly seven months along, and it seemed as if the baby was growing by leaps and bounds now. Soon, she feared, she'd be unable to get up without assistance. Of course, with no husband to help, she'd have to manage, wouldn't she?

"Time to put your drawing materials away, *dochter*. We have errands to run."

Susie looked up. "Where are we going?"

"To the bank and then to shop for baking supplies."

"You're making money like *Dat* did," Susie said with a little furrow between her brows.

"Something like that," Lucy said, "except I can bake, make money *and* stay home with you."

Her daughter grinned. "How about cookies, *Mam*?" She stood and placed her crayons and paper into a plastic bin on the table. Then she brushed off her knees and the back of her dress. "You can sell your chocolate chip cookies. And I can help you make them. We can make sugar cookies and snickerdoodles, too."

Lucy grinned. "You like my cookies, little one?"

"Gabriel calls me 'little one.'"

"He does." She felt a pang in the area near her heart.

"Ja." Susie crawled onto the chair next to her mother. "Why hasn't he come to see us?"

She tore out the check and closed her checkbook.

"I'm sure he's busy," she said. "Probably making wooden things."

"Like what?" Susie climbed to her knees and leaned over the kitchen table, turning her head to lie against the wood to face her mother.

"Toys and vegetable bins." Lucy laughed and stood, urging her daughter to sit properly in her chair with gentle hands. "He sells them in stores on consignment. Like how I sell my baked goods."

Lucy put the check with her checkbook in her purse. "We'll take the wagon to the bank, then we'll come back to make cookies, a couple of apple pies and a chocolate cake."

Susie scrambled down from her chair. "And we can make whoopie pies! I like whoopie pies."

Lucy's gaze dropped to her daughter's bare feet. "Can you find your sneakers for me, please?"

Susie ran off then returned with her sneakers and handed them to her mother. She sat in a chair and extended her legs to make it easier for Lucy to put them on.

Lucy slipped the shoes on her daughter's feet and tied them. "You need to practice tying your laces, *dochter.*"

"Ja, Mam."

When they were ready to leave, Lucy went to the paddock fence to coax Blackie closer with a carrot. Blackie looked in her direction then went back to eating grass. She sighed and tried again.

"Blackie!" Lucy raised the hand with the carrot. Her gelding turned its head and moved in her direction. "Thunder," she murmured. "I wasn't calling you." She smiled as Thunder came up to her. "But you'll do."

She watched the horse take the treat like a gentleman. "Ready to take us to the bank, boy?" She rubbed his nose then grabbed hold of his halter and tugged him toward the barn, grimacing when the movement hurt her arm. As much as she wanted to, she couldn't hitch up her horse, not when the simple action of leading him inside had caused her arm to ache and her wrist to throb again. Frustrated, she took Susie by the hand and headed back toward the house. "We're going to wait to do errands, *dochter.*"

Susie looked up at her mother. "How come?"

"It's better if we go later," Lucy told her.

She saw her cell phone on the counter as she entered the house. Gabriel had told her to call him day or night. Should she? Lucy hated the idea, especially after she'd embarrassed herself on Sunday by getting sick in front of him.

After an inner debate, she called him. Her heart raced as the call went through.

He answered on the first ring. "Lucy, are you *oll recht*?"

"I'm fine, Gabriel, but…" She paused. "I could use a little help. I don't need it right away. I need to hitch my horse to my wagon, but with my arm I can't manage—"

"I'll be right there."

"*Nay!* You don't have to come just now!" she exclaimed with dismay, but he had hung up the phone.

Within minutes, Lucy heard the sound of buggy wheels in her driveway. She hurried outside and watched as Gabriel parked his vehicle and hopped out, then headed toward the house.

* * *

"I could have waited," Lucy said with a scowl.

"Morning, Lucy," Gabriel greeted with a nod. "'Tis nice to see you, too."

"*Gut* morning," she mumbled, but he noticed the moment she couldn't contain her grin.

Susie ran out of the house. "Gabriel!"

He crouched to the little girl's level. Excited, Susie flung herself into his arms and wrapped her own around his neck.

"*Hallo*, little one," he said with a smile. Pain shot down his leg as he tried to lift her and stand. Resisting the urge to rub it, he gave up, giving her one more hug before he rose stiffly to his feet. Thankfully for him, the pain dissipated to a bearable ache. "How are you?"

"I've been drawing pictures. Want to see?" Susie grabbed his hand and started to tug him toward the house and Lucy.

"Wait," Gabriel said, halting. "I have something in my buggy for you."

Susie's eyes widened. "For me?"

"*Ja.*" He reached into the back of his buggy and pulled out a wooden toy.

"What is it?" she whispered, enthralled.

"It's a waddling duck toy."

He moved the two pieces of the toy closer and set up the wooden track. "See this duck?" he asked, watching her closely, loving the look on her face. The child nodded vigorously. "You can make him waddle down this ramp." He met Lucy's gaze with a smile before turning his attention back to Susie and the toy. "Watch, little one." He placed the toy on the front seat of his buggy and showed her how it worked. The little girl cried out with delight as the wooden duck waddled down the track.

"Can I try?" Susie asked, her pale blue eyes glistening with excitement.

"*Ja*. It's yours to keep and use whenever you like."

Lucy's adorable daughter set the duck at the top of the track with her little fingers and laughed as it waddled down its entire length. "See, *Mam*? I made him do it!"

"I see, *dochter. Wunderbor gut.*" Lucy gave him a look of gratitude as her child continued to play with her new toy.

Gabriel felt his stomach flutter when she smiled at him. She silently mouthed, *Danki*, and he grinned at her, pleased.

Susie continued to play with the toy, expressing her delight each time the duck waddled from the top of the track to the bottom. Suddenly, the child stopped and looked at him with love in her eyes that floored him. Scar or not, stranger or not, Susie accepted him for who he was, not how he looked. He felt overwhelmed by emotion as he picked up the duck and sent it waddling down the track again. "I'm going to put this in the *haus*," she said as she grabbed it before running inside.

Gabriel turned to Lucy as soon as Susie was inside. "Where do you need to go?"

"I'm fine to drive," she told him. "If you'll hitch up my horse for me, I can run errands."

He eyed her with disapproval. "Lucy," he said with great patience, "where do you need to go?"

She sighed heavily. "Just the bank…and the store. I need baking supplies." She hesitated. "I sold everything on consignment."

"That's *wunderbor*." He smiled at her with approval. His gaze captured and held hers a long time, making him feel warm and giddy. "I'll take you wherever you need to go."

"What I really need is my buggy. Eli from the carriage shop left a message at King's that he finished fixing it."

He frowned as he pushed back the brim of his black-banded straw hat. "Are you going to send him a check? We can have Bert's friend pick it up and bring it back for you."

"That makes sense," she said.

Gabriel waited for Susie to return. "I'll take you to the bank and store." He sighed heavily when she didn't answer him. "Lucy."

"Fine." She looked tired, and he realized she didn't have the energy to argue. "I should go to the bank first."

He nodded, gazing at her with tenderness, and the look in her eyes gave him pause. "You used your cell phone."

She blushed. *"Ja."*

He was pleased. "I'm glad you called." He gazed at her carefully. "You look much better. Your color is *gut*."

Lucy averted her gaze. She was likely embarrassed remembering their last time together.

Susie came outside again. She reached her mother's side then glanced curiously between the two adults. "What are you talking about?"

Lucy flashed him a look. "Gabriel is going to take us shopping."

Susie groaned. "Not for cell phones."

Gabriel laughed. *"Nay,* we already have our phones."

"When are we going?" her daughter asked with raised eyebrows.

"As soon as I get my purse." After one last look at Gabriel, who smiled at her reassuringly, she hurried into the house.

When she returned with her purse over her left arm, Gabriel was deep in a conversation with Susie, but they immediately stopped talking when they saw her.

Lucy narrowed her eyes. "What's going on?" Her daughter wore a cute little smirk. She switched her attention to Gabriel with raised eyebrows. Gabriel shook his head but continued to smile. "What are you two planning?"

"Are you ready to go?" Gabriel said, unwilling to answer.

Susie tugged on her arm and grabbed Gabriel's with her other hand. "Come on before it's lunchtime and I get hungry." She pulled them toward his buggy.

Lucy exchanged amused looks with Gabriel. He felt eager to spend the day with her.

"Do you have your phone?" Gabriel asked softly.

"In my purse," she said, patting it.

He nodded in approval as he allowed Susie to pull him toward his vehicle.

"*Mam*, can I sit in the front?"

"I think you should sit in the back, little one," Gabriel said with a smile.

"Listen to Gabriel, *dochter*. It's his buggy."

"*Oll recht,*" Susie said with a little pout. She obeyed and climbed into the back, then tugged on the back of Gabriel's shirt. "I love my duck toy. *Danki*, Gabriel."

"You're *willkomm*, little one." He climbed into the driver's seat.

Danki, she mouthed, and the look in her eyes made his heart trip.

The mailman stopped and put mail in Lucy's mailbox. "Can we stop so I can get my mail?" Lucy asked.

"*Ja*, of course." He stopped the horse before the buggy was close to the road. "I'll get it," he said, before getting out and retrieving her mail.

"Gabriel." She shook her head as he handed her the small bundle of mail.

"It was no problem, Lucy. You're *willkomm*," he teased and chuckled when she blushed.

As Gabriel drove her to the bank, Lucy looked through her mail. She flipped through the stack easily, then paused a long moment to stare at an envelope.

"Something wrong?" he asked her with concern, feeling her sudden tension.

She shoved the envelope between the others. "*Nay*, everything is fine."

He frowned, suspecting there was something that was not fine, but he couldn't make her tell him.

In the bank parking lot, Lucy climbed out at the front door of the brick building. "I won't be but a minute," she said before she headed in.

Gabriel waited patiently with Susie for Lucy to return. He felt fortunate to have this time with her and Susie. He turned to see what Susie was doing, and she smiled at him. He grinned back and then watched through the windshield as Lucy left the bank and approached. The sight of her warmed him from the inside out. He started to move to help her, but she climbed in before he had a chance.

She slid onto the seat next to him and handed him cash. "For the cell phone and fees," she said.

He frowned. "Luce, this is too much money."

Lucy shook her head. "Take it, Gabriel. I'm only paying my fair share. Friends don't take advantage of other friends."

Gabriel sighed. He couldn't argue with that.

Chapter Ten

Unlike the tense ride home from church on Sunday, the drive from the bank to the store to pick up groceries was filled with Susie's laughter and chatter with the man in the driver's seat. Though finding a letter in the mail had shaken her. What could her father possibly want? She hadn't heard from him in over four years.

A male chuckle drew her attention. What a lovely sound, Lucy thought. She found herself relaxing as she glanced at the man beside her. Gabriel looked wonderful in his spring green shirt, black tri-blend pants with black suspenders and shoes. The color of his shirt brought out the warm rich tones of his stunning brown eyes, now filled with amused fondness for her daughter.

It was a beautiful June day. A warm breeze wafted in through the sides of the vehicle, teasing his face and Lucy's *kapp* strings. He kept his attention on the road, but she felt it when he stole quick glances at her.

They visited King's General Store first. Lucy entered the store and went to grab a market basket but chose a shopping cart instead. She started down the baking aisle with Susie and Gabriel following closely.

She grabbed flour, sugar, vanilla, baking powder, chocolate chips and unsweetened baking chocolate. She heard her daughter chatting nonstop and she thought she heard Aaron's name. Or was she mistaken? Susie wouldn't have mentioned him unless Aaron was here. Lucy looked around the store and was grateful when she didn't see him.

"Do you need eggs or milk?" Gabriel asked quietly a few moments later as he came up to stand beside her.

She smiled at him. "Both."

"I'll get them for you," he said before he walked away.

The smile left Lucy's face as she watched him go. It seemed as if something was bothering him. Had he guessed that she'd been upset by the letter she'd received in the mail? She studied him when he returned with the eggs and milk and put them in her cart. "Gabriel?" He looked at her without expression. "Is something wrong?"

"What could be wrong?" he said without expression.

She frowned. "You tell me."

He shook his head. "Not now."

She felt something hard sink in her chest. Gabriel had seemed fine when he'd picked her up. In fact, he'd appeared so fast after she'd called him that she'd been startled. So maybe it did have to do with the letter. Or was it something else?

Lucy took a calming breath then finished her shopping and paid for her purchases.

Soon they were on their way back to her house.

"You're *orrig* quiet," Lucy commented for his ears only minutes later as he drove his buggy onto her property. "Are you going to tell me what's bothering you?"

He shrugged as he parked close to the hitching post near the house. "Stay where you are please." He got out and tied up his horse then came around to help Lucy get down from the carriage.

She braced herself with her hands on his shoulders for support as Gabriel lifted her down. While he reached for Susie, Lucy grabbed her mail from the floor of the buggy and clutched it against her.

"*Danki* for coming to my rescue again," she said.

"You're *willkomm*." He studied her without smiling. "If you need anything else, please let me know. Would you like me to call Bert to arrange for his friend to get your buggy?"

Lucy nodded. "That would be *wunderbor*." She didn't want him to leave, but she needed a private moment to read her father's letter. She could tell him later, when she was ready, after supper. She debated as she stared down at her shoes, before looking up and locking gazes with him. "Would you like to come back for supper? At five thirty?"

He didn't immediately respond. "That would be nice."

She felt instant relief. "Do you like fried chicken?"

"I do, but I don't remember the last time I had it." He smiled at Susie with warmth. "Be a *gut* girl for your *mudder*, little one." His smile for Lucy was less warm. "I should get going. I'll see you at five thirty." He paused. "If you're sure you want me to come."

"Of course I want you to come." She lowered her voice so that Susie wouldn't hear her. "I wouldn't have invited you if I didn't."

His expression softened as he nodded. He reached inside his buggy to get her groceries and carried them into the house for her. He set them on her kitchen table then turned to leave. "I'll see you later," he said softly.

"*Mam?* Where is Gabriel going?" Susie asked as Lucy watched him leave.

"Home, Susie. But he'll be back later to have supper with us."

"Bye, Gabriel!" Lucy's daughter called out through the screen.

"I'll see you later, little one," he said with a wave.

When he was gone, Lucy ushered Susie farther into the house and closed the door. "Why don't you lie down for a little while? I'm going to rest, too, after I put away the groceries and read the mail," she said as she started to unpack the grocery bags. "We can eat something later."

"Can I lie down with you?" Susie asked, pleading with her big blue eyes.

"Go ahead and lie in my bed. I'll come up soon. I have to do something before I join you. You'll have to try your best to sleep, *ja?*"

"I will." Susie grabbed the duck toy from the kitchen table. "I'll just put this in my room first."

After making sure the house was locked, Lucy sat at the table and stared at her father's handwriting on the envelope. Her heart raced as she wondered what he had to say. She was afraid to open it. He had hurt her badly, and couldn't imagine why he'd felt the need to write to her. Had he recently read about Harley's death in *The Budget*, the Amish newspaper? Maybe he had sent condolences. She shook her head. *Nay*, that wasn't something her father would do. He didn't care enough about her to worry over her as a widow. Which meant he wanted something from her.

She tore open the envelope, pulled out the letter inside. She felt sick to her stomach as she hesitated to unfold it and read what her father had written. Lucy drew a sharp breath, unfolded the letter and began to read.

> *Lucy,*
> *Mari is pregnant. I need you to come home to help her. Harley can take of his dochter or you can ask that sister of his to watch the girl. I'll expect to see you soon. I am your dat. Do not disappoint me.*
> *Your vadder*

"Nay, *Vadder*, I'm not coming. I'm pregnant, a widow, and I have a *dochter* who I love and appreciate, unlike you do your *dochter*—me," she muttered. "You didn't care when I left. You may be my *vadder* but I don't owe you anything." She tried to block out the guilt. "I did everything I could for you, and it wasn't enough until I left like you wanted me to." She shook her head. "You should have known about Harley's death, but apparently, *Vadder*, you don't care enough about anyone else to read our Amish newspaper, *The Budget*."

In the past, Lucy would never have thought she would disobey her father, but his actions and his coldness toward her had changed all that. Her life was here now, and she was staying. He'd have to find someone else to help his young pregnant wife. The only person she missed back in Ohio was her little brother. Was Seth well? Was their father being good to him? Did he care for his son? She hoped so. He'd never cared for her.

She had written to her brother several times over the years with no answer. Seth had been only nine years old when she'd left. He would be thirteen now, almost a man. She'd wanted to visit Seth, to make sure he was all right, but Harley hadn't allowed it. She was not to interfere with a man's raising of his son, Harley had hold her. Still, Lucy had remained worried about leaving her sweet little brother in the hands of her father and his new wife.

She refolded her father's letter and slipped it back into the envelope. She would write back to him later, after she rested. With her mind made up to reject her father's offer, she felt relieved as she climbed the stairs. She was tired and more than ready for a nap.

When Lucy woke up from her nap, she felt more rested. She looked at her watch and saw that she'd slept for an hour and a half. She sat up and smiled to see Susie still sleeping beside her.

She got up carefully and went downstairs. She told Gabriel that she'd make fried chicken for supper, and there was plenty of time before she'd have to cook the chicken. It was best if it was freshly fried and hot right before eating it.

Lucy made herself a quick cup of tea and ventured into the great room to enjoy the quiet for a few minutes. Her mind settled on her father, and she forced her disappointment with him away. As she sipped from the hot brew, she thought of Gabriel. Something had been bothering him even before he'd given her the mail. What?

Lucy was intensely curious about him. She wanted to ask how he had gotten his facial scar. About his family. And his sister, whom she'd met briefly. Emily had been pleasant, although Lucy hadn't spent much time in her company since she'd left early on Sunday the way she had.

Where were Gabriel's parents? Did he have other siblings? Where did Gabriel and Emily live before coming to New Berne? Did they like living here?

She'd only known the man a short time, but she felt extremely comfortable in Gabriel's presence. She liked him. A lot. Gabriel was the direct opposite of Harley. Nor was he like Aaron. And he most definitely was not like her father.

Gabriel Fisher was someone special.

Lucy took a sip from her tea, allowing its warmth to slide down her throat and soothe her wayward thoughts. She carried her tea as she went through the kitchen and stepped outside. The afternoon sun was warm and felt good against her skin. The scent of the flowers she'd planted along the side of the house and up to the porch reached out with their perfume. She loved spring and early summer, which started next week.

Lucy finished her tea then got to work. She took the chicken out of the refrigerator and cut it into frying-size pieces. Then she grabbed some potatoes from the pantry closet and scrubbed them in the sink, then cut them into small chunks and covered them with water in a pan. After setting it aside to boil later, she dumped a jar of sweet and sour canned mixed garden vegetables into a bowl and put it into the refrigerator. Then she assembled the ingredients for the cobbler crust before she opened the jar of peaches, drained the juice into a bowl and stirred cinnamon and sugar into the fruit.

As she prepared the dessert, someone knocked on her side door. She glanced through the glass, surprised to see Aaron.

"Lucy?"

She opened the door but didn't let him inside. "What are you doing here, Aaron?"

"I just wanted to check up on you."

She sighed. "I understand that you and Harley were best friends, but your checking up on me has to stop. We talked about this on Sunday."

Aaron nodded. "I know, but—"

"I think you need to stay away," Lucy said, interrupting him. First her father's letter and now this visit. She'd had enough. "You can see Susie on Sundays after church service."

"Lucy." When she remained firm, he sighed. "I'm sorry."

"Don't be sorry, Aaron. Just go."

She watched him leave with a new sense of freedom. She was done being manipulated by the men in her life. It was time to fully take charge of herself, to do what she wanted and needed—within the bounds of the Amish community.

She felt a sudden sharp longing for Gabriel, wishing he'd come early. He never made her feel anything less than who she was. Lucy realized with a shock that she felt safe and loved with him. Did he feel it, too? If she could figure out what was bothering him, then maybe they would have a chance at more than friendship. Unless what was bothering him was that he'd guessed she had feelings for him and he didn't return them.

She put the peaches in the refrigerator and the ingredients for the crust away. She would serve peaches with ice cream and forget the cobbler.

"Mam?"

"Did you have a good sleep?" Lucy asked softly when her daughter entered the kitchen, rubbing her eyes.

Susie bobbed her head. "What time are we going to eat?"

"Soon. Gabriel is coming to supper."

She suddenly looked excited. "I forgot! Can I set the table?"

"I'd like that." Lucy put plates, napkins and forks within her reach. She watched with affection as Susie folded the napkins set them next to each plate.

"Is Gabriel here?"

"Not yet," Lucy said. "I have an idea. Why don't you get your duck toy and play with it in the great room until Gabriel gets here? I think he would love to see you play with it."

"Oll recht." Susie went upstairs to get the duck from her room.

A second buggy appeared in her driveway. Gabriel's. He stepped down from his vehicle and approached the house. Her gaze took in every aspect of him, from his black-banded straw hat to his royal blue shirt with black pants held up by black suspenders.

She felt a jolt when he locked eyes with her. She was suddenly afraid. She was starting to fall for this man and didn't know how he felt about her.

As he reached the house, Gabriel saw the door open. Lucy stood, a breathtaking sight in a bright blue dress with her white prayer *kapp* covering her dark hair. Her eyes were a vivid blue, and they were filled with emotion. He halted and froze. It looked like she might have deep feelings for him. He was afraid to hope, because despite the way he'd felt earlier when he'd left, he'd done a lot of thinking. And the only conclusion he'd come to was that Lucy meant much more to him than his former betrothed.

He smiled and continued until he reached her. She held the door open and he stepped inside. "*Hallo*, Lucy," he greeted softly, pleased by the look in her eyes. He stepped inside the house and dared to take her hand, interlocking his fingers with hers. He knew she didn't mind when her eyes brightened as he gave her fingers a gentle squeeze before releasing them. "How are you, Luce?"

"Better now that you're here," she murmured as she led him through the kitchen.

"Are you going to talk to me this evening?"

She nodded. "After Susie's in bed. Can you stay?"

"I can stay," he said, pleased that she wanted him to.

"Susie's in the great room," she explained. "She couldn't wait for you to get here."

Gabriel grinned. "She is a special little girl," he whispered, his heart full.

Her expression warmed as she took him into the other room where her daughter was. "I'm going to put on the chicken," she said. "It won't take long."

Joy settling in his chest, Gabriel gazed at her with tenderness. "Lucy—" he began.

"Gabriel!" Susie exclaimed happily, interrupting, drawing his attention. Lucy's daughter sprang to her feet and ran to him. "You came!"

He grinned at her welcome. "I did. You seem glad to see me."

"I am! I've been waiting all afternoon for you to come." She gestured toward her toys on the floor. "Look! I'm playing with my duck! See?"

"I'm happy you like it, Susie." He could feel Lucy

observing them closely. He met her gaze, saw her blush and look away. He couldn't remember a time when he'd felt this kind of excitement, this hope.

"Gabriel, do you want to play with me?" Susie asked.

"*Dochter*, Gabriel just got here," Lucy told her. "Let's go into the kitchen and you can play on the floor where he can relax and watch you."

Minutes later Gabriel alternately watched Susie play and Lucy put on supper. She turned on the heat under the potatoes and warmed oil in a frying pan. The kitchen was soon filled with the scent of the fried chicken. His stomach grumbled as he watched Lucy turn the chicken in the sizzling grease until each piece was crispy. When the chicken was ready, she removed the pieces from the pan and placed them on a paper towel to remove some of the grease before setting them on a large plate. She finished mashing the potatoes, then spooned them into a bowl before she set everything on the kitchen table.

They sat down to eat, and he thought of how much they were like a family, eating together, talking about ordinary things. After dinner, Lucy got up to clear the table and Gabriel rose to help her.

"You don't have to do that," she said with surprise.

"You don't want my help?" He stiffened and met her eyes.

She looked stunned and grateful. "It's not that," she explained hesitantly.

"Then what is it?" He softened his expression as he stood close to her, holding the dish of leftover mashed potatoes. He lowered his voice. "Your husband didn't…"

Lucy stole a glance at Susie, who had climbed down from her chair to help. She took the dish from Gabriel and reached up on her toes to put it on the kitchen counter.

"Lucy, why are you surprised by my help?"

"*Dat* never helped her," Susie said matter-of-factly as she turned and went back to the table to collect the paper napkins.

"Susie," she began, looking horrified at what her daughter had said—and feeling even more surprised she had noticed at such a young age—until she realized that Susie didn't think anything less of her father for not helping. It was just the way he was. She'd felt so uncomfortable under Harley's scrutiny that she'd wanted only to escape. Like many Amish men, her late husband had adhered to a strict division of duties within the household.

Gabriel hadn't moved. Lucy saw his face had become unreadable as he waited for her to explain. *Can I tell you later?* she mouthed to him.

He nodded, then picked up the meat platter and placed it next to the bowl of potatoes. They cleaned up after dinner in silence.

"It's a nice night," Gabriel said after the dishes were washed and put away. He had dried after she'd washed. Lucy had been amazed at his willingness to help with "women's work." He smiled at Susie, who was cuddling her doll on the linoleum floor. "Shall we sit outside on your front porch?"

Lucy nodded. *"Oll recht."*

She gazed at her daughter lovingly. "Susie, would you like to play on the front porch for a while before bed?"

"Gabriel, are you coming, too?" She sprang to her feet.

He lifted her into his arms. "*Ja*, I wouldn't have it any other way."

Susie grinned at him, displaying little even teeth, as she patted his right cheek. "I like it on the porch. We don't sit there much." She struggled to get down, and he released her. Susie picked up her doll, clutching it to her. "You used to sit outside with *Vadder* sometimes, didn't you, *Mam*?"

Lucy froze. Had Susie heard her and her father talking? "Sometimes," she admitted, afraid that she'd heard Harley's loud, hurtful voice complaining about her mother.

"We don't have to sit outside," Gabriel said quietly, watching her closely as if he'd sensed her unease.

She made a genuine effort to smile. "*Nay*, 'tis a beautiful evening. We can enjoy dessert outside. Are you ready for peaches and ice cream?"

"*Ja!*" Susie cried as she raced to her mother to hug her. "I can't put my arms around you, *Mam*. Your belly is getting bigger and bigger."

Blushing, Lucy stole a glance at Gabriel. "I love peaches and ice cream," he said.

"When is the baby coming?" her daughter asked, still holding on to Lucy.

"Not for a while yet." She saw him stifle a smile.

A few minutes later, she and Gabriel sat side by side in porch rockers, eating dessert, while little Susie sat on the top step, enjoying hers, as well.

"Can I have more?" Susie asked, turning to show a mouth covered with vanilla ice cream.

"Tomorrow, after you eat all your lunch," Lucy said.

"Can Gabriel come over and have more, too?"

"He's always welcome." Lucy stole a glance and was pleased to see Gabriel's smile.

"This dessert is too *gut* to not come back for more," he said with amusement.

"Susie, *dochter*, time for bed. Go upstairs and wash up. I'll be up shortly to help you get ready."

After handing over her plate to Lucy, Susie rushed to open the door, pausing after she swung it wide. "I'll see you tomorrow, Gabriel."

He nodded. "Sleep well, little one." His voice was soft, his expression tender. He captured Lucy's gaze and she exchanged smiles with him while Susie entered the house and ran upstairs.

"I'll get her into bed and then…" Her voice trailed off. She felt suddenly nervous at the prospect of the conversation they were bound to have.

He reached for her and Susie's plates. "I'll wash these for you."

"You don't have to," she objected but stopped and relented when she saw his face. *"Danki."*

Gabriel couldn't remember the last time he'd enjoyed himself more. Before the fire, he realized with amazement. Mother and daughter were beautiful and precious, and he hoped that Lucy returned even a fraction of what he felt for her. Still, there was the matter of Aaron Hostetler. He needed to know how big a part of her life Aaron was, if Emily's fears that Aaron cared too much for Lucy were valid.

He washed and dried the dessert dishes, then put them away where they belonged. Lucy came into the kitchen as he was putting the leftover peaches into the refrigerator.

"Gabriel," she breathed.

He reached for her hand. "I enjoy helping you, Luce." He ran his gaze over her pretty features, appreciating her as he so often did. Today, her bright blue dress matched the azure color of her captivating eyes. "Would you like to sit outside?" he asked quietly.

Soft, silky eyelashes flickered against her cheeks, drawing attention to their rich dark color. Her nose was small and slightly pointed at the tip. Her mouth, a dark natural pink, was perfectly shaped with a lovely dip in the center of her upper lip. "We can sit on the front porch," she agreed. "Susie is already asleep, despite taking a nap this afternoon."

He continued to study her, fascinated with her face, the color of her eyes, the way she came up to his chin when she stood. "Lucy…"

She blushed. "Did you want something more to drink? Coffee? Tea?"

He curved his lips slowly upward. "*Nay.* You?"

Lucy shrugged. "Not really."

Gabriel shook his head. "Let's just sit for a bit, then."

At her nod, he took her hand and led her outside, releasing her to sit before he took the other chair. She stilled when he shifted his rocking chair closer.

"I have to ask you something, and I don't want you to take this the wrong way," he began.

She nodded. "What is it?"

"Aaron Hostetler."

She froze. "What about him?"

Tension radiated from her, increasing his. "Are you and he…"

Lucy jerked. *"Nay!"*

"My sister Emily cares for him. They've been seeing

each other for weeks now, but she thinks that he canceled supper with her because of you."

She grew quiet and looked reflective as he studied her. "Aaron was my husband's best friend. After Harley died, he was there for Susie and me. It was fine, at first, but then he wouldn't stop coming around, worrying about me. I told him to stop but he wouldn't. I couldn't understand why. Until Sunday."

He could tell she was upset. "What happened on Sunday?" he asked quietly.

"He told me he needed to take care of me. That I should marry him. I told him I wouldn't. I didn't need him, and he needed to live his life."

Gabriel frowned. "He said he wanted to marry you."

"He did, at first, but then I found out why. It's not because he wants to marry me. It's because he blames himself for Harley's death. Apparently, Harley took his place in the truck that had the accident, while Aaron stayed on the job longer and went home with another crew."

"So he felt responsible for you." He glanced away, his thoughts processing what she'd said.

"And there was more," Lucy said, drawing his glance. "About six months ago, Harley came home from the job drunk. He'd gone out with the English crew. He'd been upset since the night before. He was upset with me." She stopped, looked away.

He reached out, captured her hand. "Why?"

"Harley loved Susie's mother. He—" He could feel her embarrassment.

"Six months ago," he echoed. He blinked in sudden understanding. Her baby. "He felt guilty after being with you."

She wouldn't look at him, wouldn't answer him, but he knew it was true. "So Aaron..." he prompted, hoping to move them forward. She should never be embarrassed with him.

"Ja," she said. "Harley came home drunk. I was making dinner. Fried chicken." Her smile for him was wry. "He wanted my attention and in his eagerness, he grabbed the knife I was using and—"

Gabriel gaped at her. "Did he hurt you?"

"It was an accident. The slice on my arm was just an accident, and Harley felt terrible. He was so sorry, he cried like a baby. After that, he retreated to the way he was when I first married him. Alone and distant. Only with Susie did he show any warmth."

He reached out, touched her cheek and stroked it with his finger. She briefly closed her eyes. "I'm sorry." He withdrew his hand.

"Why? You didn't do anything wrong."

"I'm sorry that you had to go through that." It bothered him.

"I got Susie out of my marriage so I consider everything I went through worth it." She smiled. "May I ask you something?" When he nodded, she said, "Where did you move from?"

"Ohio."

"You and Emily." She tilted her head as she considered him. "What about the rest of your family? Your parents?"

He stiffened but answered her. "Dead."

She gasped. *"Ach nay,* Gabriel. I'm so sorry. I didn't know."

He gave her a weak smile. "How could you?"

"How?" she breathed, almost as if she was afraid to ask.

"House fire. They all died in a house fire."

Lucy eyed him with a soft expression. She reached out and touched his facial scar. "Is that how you got this?"

He nodded. "That and worse," he admitted. He had to tell her, if he ever wanted a future with her. For some reason, it felt like she was the only one he could tell.

"Where?" she asked, her voice soft, her eyes glistening. When he didn't immediately answer her, she shifted in her chair. "Your leg," she guessed. "I saw the way you limp sometimes. 'Tis your left leg, *ja*?"

"*Ja*, it was—is—bad."

Lucy saw the pain in Gabriel's eyes as he talked about his leg. She suspected there was more he hadn't told her yet, and she wanted to know. Not because it would make a difference in how she felt about him, but because she wanted—needed—to make him feel better, if she could. "Was Emily hurt in the fire?"

"*Nay*, I got her out first."

"You tried to rescue the others," she said, watching as his expression mirrored his pain.

He nodded. "I brought my little *bruder* out next, but David was dead. Smoke inhalation, they told me."

"Oh, Gabriel…" She shifted her chair closer, slipped her arm around his. He tried to withdraw from her, but she wouldn't let him.

He shuddered out a sigh. "I tried to go back in for the others, but the fire department had arrived and wouldn't let me. My pant leg was on fire. I didn't realize—didn't care. I only wanted to save my parents, my older *bruder* and *schweschter*, and my *mam* and *dat*."

She stood and moved behind him, slipped her arms around his shoulders, leaning in close so that she could listen closely to the sound of his harsh breathing.

"How long were you in the hospital?" she asked, closing her eyes.

"Weeks. It was…"

"Terrible," she supplied for him.

"*Ja*, I had third-degree burns on my thigh and second-degree burns from my knee to my ankle. The burn treatments were…bad," he admitted. "The second-degree burns wouldn't heal and ended up needing skin graft surgeries to replace the damaged skin on my leg. Not all of them took, and I had to go in for another one."

She felt his pain and found herself silently crying. "I'm sorry."

He pulled forward and glanced back at her, seeming stunned by the sight of her tears. "Lucy…"

"I care for you, Gabriel. I know we haven't known each other long, but I've never felt this way about anyone before."

He stared at her. "You do?" When she nodded, he briefly closed his eyes. "I feel something, too, Lucy."

She stepped back and returned to her chair. She gazed at him with love, feeling happiness beyond anything she'd ever known. He had shared something painful, which made her feel closer to him. She wiped her eyes. "Gabriel, I…what can I do to help?"

His brown eyes glistening, he cracked a small smile. "I could use a cup of coffee."

Chapter Eleven

Minutes later, Lucy sat with him on the front porch as they sipped coffee.

Gabriel was silent as he drank from his mug in the chair beside hers. The brew had eased the lump in his throat that had risen as he'd recalled the terrifying moments of the fire. It was a lovely night, and he felt... refreshed. He'd told her about the fire and his leg, and she had been supportive, loving. Lucy was a woman he could take a chance with, he realized. He closed his eyes briefly before opening them to focus on her.

"Gabriel..."

"Tell me about the letter you received today."

She stiffened but then relaxed with a little sigh. "It was from my *vadder*."

He frowned. "Why did a letter from your *dat* upset you?"

"Because it was the first time I've heard from him since I married Harley over four years ago."

His expression went soft, his brown eyes filled with compassion. "Tell me why."

"He arranged my marriage to Harley. My *mudder*

died only a few months before, and he wanted me out of the way so that he could marry again."

Gabriel furrowed his brow as he studied her. "I don't understand."

"Because his new wife didn't want me there." Lucy stared into the distance. "His wife, my stepmother, was only a year older than I was."

He gazed at her with shock. "I see why that's upsetting." He reached out for her hand again. "Do you have any *bruders* and *schweschters*?"

"One *bruder*. Seth. He was only nine when I left. Apparently, Mari didn't have a problem with him living in the *haus* with them." Her tone was filled with such pain that he longed to take her fully into his arms and hug her.

"Lucy."

"I'm *oll recht*," she assured him. "I didn't want to marry Harley, but my father told me I had to." She stopped, as if unwilling to discuss the pain of her only living parent's betrayal. Releasing a sharp breath, she shifted in her chair to face him. "If I didn't, I'd have to fend for myself. I was too embarrassed to tell anyone. So I married Harley for Susie. She was a beautiful, tiny *bubbel* when I first saw her. Only two weeks old. Harley had come to Indiana because his wife Fannie was originally from our Amish community. He wanted to show his in-laws their *dochter's* baby. Only Fannie's parents were no longer living there. His brother-in-law Abe was, however, and Abe suggested that Harley marry quickly so the baby would have a mother. Harley couldn't earn a living *and* take care of his child. Abe knew my *dat*, and he met with him to discuss the idea of marrying me to Harley. My *vadder*…was receptive."

Gabriel frowned. "I bet his was."

Lucy looked away. "The marriage was beneficial to everyone."

"You, too?"

"Only because I became Susie's *mam*."

"Let's stand a moment," Gabriel said. He stood, held out his hand. When she placed her hand in his, he smiled and pulled her to her feet. He led her to the porch railing to look out over her front yard and the trees on the other side of the lawn that concealed her house from the road.

She relaxed as she leaned against the railing with a sigh. The scents of late spring were more noticeable this evening—the rosebushes along the front had bloomed, filling the evening air with the white, red and bright pink blossoms' sweet smell. Gabriel shifted to stand behind her and rested his hands on each side of her on the railing, caging her within the circle of his arms. She inhaled sharply but didn't try to break free.

She caught a faint whiff of Gabriel's soap and the pleasing scent of the outdoors that emanated from him. The sun had dipped low in the sky, casting a glow as it made the transition from day to night. The light played over the porch, surrounding them with soft golden light. She could see clearly the tiny hairs on the back of his arms below his short shirtsleeves.

"Why did your *vadder* write to you, Lucy?"

She stiffened. "He wants me to come for an extended visit."

"Are you going to go?"

"Nay."

"Why not?"

Lucy tensed, stiffening, before she looked at him briefly over her shoulder. "Do you think I should consider it?"

"*Nay*, unless you want to."

"I don't." She tried to move away, but he soothed her with a soft touch on her shoulder.

"I only ask because he's your *vadder*, your only living parent," he pointed out gently. "It would be natural for you to want to see him, mend the rift between you." He trailed his fingers down her nape. "I know he hurt you."

"He doesn't want me to visit him to fix our relationship, Gabriel. He wants me to come home to work. To take care of his pregnant wife."

She heard him inhale sharply. "That's…"

"Wrong," she said. Her throat tightened.

"Ja." He turned her to face him. *"Ja,* that's wrong." He regarded her with brown eyes filled with regret. "I'm sorry. I lost my parents, and they were wonderful people who loved all of us. I can't imagine parents who aren't the same."

Lucy relaxed against the railing. "I understand. But you need to know that while my *mudder* loved my *bruder* and me, I didn't see, didn't realize, until after her death, that my *vadder* loves only himself. He is the head of the family so everything he says must be obeyed." She spun back to face the front yard. "I did obey him time and again, like a dutiful *dochter*. But I won't now. This time I will listen to my heart. This is my home. My *vadder* doesn't know Harley is dead, and it wouldn't make a difference to him if he did. In his mind, it would be more of a reason for me to come 'home.' But Indiana is not home. New Berne is."

Lucy took a moment to breathe deeply and evenly before continuing. "Do you know what else he told me? That if Harley wouldn't watch his daughter, then I should get Harley's sister to watch the girl. All my *vadder* cares about is that I come to help his pregnant wife, the same wife who supposedly didn't want me around before now. I don't think he even likes me. If he liked me at all, he would never have treated me the way he did."

He leaned close to whisper in her ear. "Lucy, I like you." She could feel his breath on her nape. "I like you a lot."

She jerked with surprise and tried to face him again, but he kept her in place then lowered his chin to her shoulder. Leaning against the railing with Gabriel at her back, she softened against him. "I like you a lot, too," she admitted in a whisper. She was quiet for several moments. "Gabriel?"

"Hmm?"

"Will you let me see your leg?" She wanted to know more about him, including the times he suffered. How could she understand fully otherwise, if she didn't know?

She felt him tense up. "I…it's bad, Lucy. I'm not sure you're ready to see it."

"Oll recht." She cared deeply for him and wouldn't push him until he was ready. And eventually he would have to be if he wanted a future with her. If that was what he intended when he'd told her he liked her. Unless it was to comfort her when she'd confessed that she didn't think her father loved her like a father should. Gabriel would love his children, she thought. He was

kind and affectionate with Susie. He would make a wonderful father.

"Let's go for a walk," he suggested.

"Are you sure you want to?" She hesitated. "Susie—"

"I'm fine." He smiled at her. "And we won't go far. We'll be able to hear her if she wakes up."

"Let's walk, then," Lucy said and reached for his arm, her fingers gripping his bicep.

They descended the porch steps into the yard. The sun had dipped lower in the sky, and he could see lightning bugs by the evergreens that lined the roadway in front of her house. Gabriel directed them to the side of the house and Lucy easily followed his lead. He stayed on her left. Reaching for her hand, he interlocked their fingers. The warmth of her hand against his heated her from the inside out. She loved spending time with him, eating and sharing secrets. He had shared something painful with her, and she had told him about her father's letter.

"Gabriel?" she asked, her voice reaching out to him in the dusk.

Thanks to Gabriel, Lucy had begun to understand that *Gott* had a plan for her, a life that had included heartache but would also give her joy.

She stepped back and held his hand, leaning against him slightly as they continued their evening stroll. They walked around, not straying far from the house. As night descended, the pain of their pasts seemed to linger in the air between them. Gabriel gave her fingers an affectionate squeeze and she felt a lightening within her heart.

She wanted to hold on to these moments with him

until they reached the point where they both felt secure with one another.

"You've become quiet," she said as they neared the porch after circling the house twice.

"Just thinking."

"About?"

He halted, touched her cheek. "You." She felt the warmth of his hand as he caressed her face before he withdrew his touch. "I should go. It's getting late."

"Ja," she breathed.

"I don't want to go, but I'll come back tomorrow… if you want."

She gave her answer by leaning into him. "I'd like that," she said.

They stood close, and he seemed as reluctant as she for the night to be over. When Gabriel kissed her cheek, she nearly swooned. *"Gut nache*, Lucy. I'll see you tomorrow afternoon. I have a delivery to make in the morning. If I get done early, I'll come sooner."

"I'll look forward to seeing you again." At his gentle urging, she climbed the steps. "Until tomorrow, Gabriel."

Gabriel carried the sweet memory of the evening with Lucy all the way home.

Emily was surprisingly awake and reading by oil lamp when he entered the house fifteen minutes later. "You've been gone a long time," she said accusingly. "You were with her again, weren't you?"

"Do you have a problem with my spending time with Lucy, *schweschter*? I thought your problem was with Lucy and Aaron together, not with her and me."

With a heavy sigh, she closed her book. "It is with her and Aaron, but it's been hard since Aaron has stayed absent."

He pulled out a chair and sat next to her. "Em, Lucy doesn't care for him. She told me that Aaron was her husband's best friend and he keeps trying to help her, but she doesn't want or need his help." He waited until she met his gaze. "Are you sure Aaron is the right man for you?"

Tears filled her eyes. "I don't know. I love him, but I'm beginning to wonder if he ever had feelings for me."

"You are a warm, *gut*-hearted woman. If not Aaron, then you will meet some other man deserving of your affections." He studied her bent head. "You look exhausted. Why don't you go to bed? Tomorrow is another day and things may look different."

Nodding, Emily rose and reached for the oil lamp. "Are you coming up?"

"In a few minutes." He stood and took a flashlight from a kitchen drawer. "Go ahead up. I've got my light to see." He switched on the light. After watching his sister leave, Gabriel poured himself a glass of milk and sat down again, his thoughts lingering on his day with Lucy, the woman he cared about. And he smiled.

After Gabriel left, Lucy was too excited to head up to bed. His friendship, his caring, made her feel good about herself. She made herself a cup of hot milk, sweetening it with sugar, then she sat in the kitchen and wrote back to her father. She didn't mention Harley's death in her letter. Her father would have pushed it as an excuse for her return to Indiana.

Dear Vadder,
I won't be returning to Indiana. My life is here
in Pennsylvania. I have a daughter to raise and
soon I'll have another baby of my own. My life
and my friends are here, and I'm not leaving.
You will have to find someone else to help Mari.
Lucy

With her letter done, she finished her warm milk,
headed up to bed and fell asleep with thoughts of the
wonderful evening spent in Gabriel's company.

The next morning at 5 a.m., she woke up refreshed
and ready for the day. The first thing she did after dress-
ing was to put a stamp on the envelope addressed to her
father and put it in the mailbox by the road. Susie was
still in bed when she returned. After a quick check on
her daughter, Lucy went to work, baking cakes, pies,
muffins and bar desserts to replace her stock at King's
and Peter's Pockets. Her buggy would be arriving today,
and she wanted all of her bakery items ready for delivery. She allowed everything to cool before she wrapped
each treat and labeled them for sale.

The sun shone through the kitchen windows, which
she opened to allow in the fresh air. Susie came downstairs at eight, and with a warning to stay put, Lucy
gave her a muffin to eat on the front porch. Basking
in the warmth and joy of the day, Lucy ate a bowl of
cornflakes then enjoyed a second cup of tea. She wondered what time this afternoon Gabriel would get here.

Suddenly, she heard the rumble of a truck coming up
her driveway. Lucy opened the side door just as the large
flatbed tow truck carrying her newly repaired buggy
pulled up alongside the house and parked.

"*Mam*, a truck is here!" Susie cried, running from the porch through the house to reach her.

"*Ja, dochter.* It's our buggy," Lucy told her, pleased with how Eli had made the vehicle look brand-new.

"It looks shiny!" Susie pushed to get past her, but Lucy grabbed her before she could run out to the truck.

She watched the men roll off her buggy. "Where to?" one asked.

Lucy gestured toward her outbuilding. "Could you put it close to the barn?"

The truck left a short time later. Lucy wanted to hitch up her horse, but she knew it would be better if she waited for Gabriel to do it for her. She couldn't stop the warm happiness that filled her up in knowing the wonderful man whose company she enjoyed so much would soon be there. They'd shared a lot with each other recently, even confessed that they liked each other. He meant a lot to her. She trusted the feeling was mutual. For a heartbreaking moment, the thought that he didn't care for her as much as she cared for him entered her mind, worrying her. Until she remembered the way he'd looked at her and held her hand as they walked together near her house, and her concern disappeared.

It was up to God to decide. If their relationship was meant to be, it would happen.

Chapter Twelve

At noon, Gabriel parked his buggy next to Lucy's. He'd woken up this morning with a painful twinge in his leg and had been quick to put on a lidocaine patch. The patch seemed to work, and thankfully the pain had dissipated as if it had never been. He got out and walked around Lucy's repaired vehicle, pleased with how wonderful it looked, almost brand-new.

Eli Lapp had done a good job. He'd have to keep the carriagemaker in mind if he ever needed work done on any of his carriages or if he wanted to purchase a new one.

He left the buggy to head toward the house then changed directions when he saw Lucy sitting outside with Susie on a quilt spread out on the grass. Mother and daughter looked beautiful with the sun shining on their smiling faces. He was overwhelmed with joy as he headed their way.

"You're here!" Susie cried when she saw him. She jumped up from the quilt and ran to meet him.

"How are my two favorite girls today?" he asked as he dared to pick up Susie, hefting her into his arms for a brief hug before setting her down. His leg didn't feel the strain under Susie's weight. The NSAIDs and the patch he wore under his pants leg did wonders for him. He'd begun to feel, to hope, that he could continue to live a pain-free life.

Studying the woman before him, he saw a beautiful soul behind a lovely face. The memory of last evening with Lucy made him happy and warm whenever he looked at her. And he said a silent prayer of thanks when he saw that delight in her bright blue eyes as they locked gazes. She was as pleased to see him as he was to see her.

With her in mind, Gabriel had dressed nicely in a bright spring green short-sleeved shirt with navy pants. He tugged off his hat and laid it along with his cell phone on the quilt before he sat down on the edge. Susie didn't join them. She ran around the backyard with excess energy. The child was a whirlwind of motion, an adorable, loving whirlwind of joyful, youthful motion.

Gabriel watched Susie for a minute before turning his attention fully to Lucy. He leaned close to her. "*Hallo*, Lucy," he murmured into her ear.

"Gabriel, you're just in time for lunch. I made extra sandwiches in case you stopped by earlier than expected."

He gave a slow smile. She jerked. "Oh!" She cradled her abdomen and laughed. When Gabriel tilted his head with curiosity, she grinned. "The baby moved." He became startled when she grabbed his hand and placed it on her belly. Her unborn daughter or son moved for him, and he widened his eyes. "Lucy," he breathed in awe.

"I know. It's amazing."

He dipped his head and didn't move his hand, startled by the intimacy and wonder of feeling the ripples that were her baby's movements. The warmth of her beneath his fingers felt alive and comfortable. They locked gazes, and with a little grin of embarrassment, he sat back, taking his hand with him.

"Gabriel, a baby isn't easy," she began as if it was something that she needed him to consider. "Not like Susie. A baby cries a lot and needs twenty-four-hour care."

"I know," he said with a small smile. "You think I've never been around a baby." He grew quiet and pain flickered across his features. "My *bruder* David," he said, "He was two years old when he died. I remember what it was like to have a *bubbel* in the *haus*."

She looked stricken. "I'm sorry."

"I'm not sorry that you're pregnant, Lucy. If we… I'd easily love your baby because the child will be yours. Don't think you having a baby will make me change my mind…you, because nothing can do that. Nothing." He paused. "Do you understand?"

Her eyes filled with tears. "I understand," she whispered.

Gabriel never expected to love again, but Lucy Schwartz turned out to be a woman he could see himself falling for. His feelings for her were stronger than what he'd ever felt for Lizzy.

Watching her, he was overwhelmed with emotion. He'd never felt a baby move inside a mother before. Some might be shocked that he and Lucy had gotten so close, but they had been through so much—in the past, before they'd met, and together. They hadn't actually exchanged words of love. Perhaps it was too soon for that, but he was falling for her.

"Susie, are you ready to eat?" Lucy called as her daughter continued to race around the yard.

Watching her with amusement, Gabriel figured she'd wear herself out and be ready for a nap not long after eating. Susie ran to the quilt and beamed at him as she sat down close to him.

"Are you going to eat with us?" she asked.

Gabriel met Lucy's gaze before he answered her daughter. *"Ja,* little one."

"Peanut butter and jelly for Susie," she declared. Lucy handed him a sandwich. "And for us, chicken salad with lettuce on white bread."

Gabriel unwrapped the sandwich and took a bite. "Best chicken salad ever," he said, closing his eyes briefly as Susie had done. *"Ja! Wunderbor gut!"* He was delighted when Lucy laughed outright.

"Danki. I'm glad you like it." Her lips curving, Lucy handed him a bottle of water.

"I like everything about you," he whispered out of Susie's earshot.

Her bright blue eyes lit up. "I feel the same…" she stole a glance at Susie, who was watching two tiny birds scuttling through the grass while she ate "…about you," Lucy breathed. "But Gabriel…"

He sighed. "I know. We've known each other only a short time."

"Ja." She looked cautious, wary, but he knew she felt the same way. She showed how much she cared about him from the look in her eyes to the warmth of her smile. They would be together, he thought. He just had to be patient.

After finishing lunch, Lucy gave out the cupcakes she'd made. Gabriel experienced a deep feeling of contentment as he ate a cupcake with Lucy and Susie. "Your buggy looks *gut*. Eli did a nice job," he said after he swallowed a delicious bite of cake.

Lucy chewed and swallowed her own bite of cake then ran her tongue over the frosting that had stuck to her upper lip. "*Ja*, they brought it this morning."

"You didn't hitch up your horse," he observed.

"*Nay*, I was waiting for you."

He grinned. "*Gut maydel!*"

She returned his grin. "I'm hardly a girl."

"That's true," he admitted. "You must be old enough to be my *grossmudder*. You're seventy-five, *ja*?" He couldn't control his smile.

She balled up her sandwich wrapper and threw it at him. "Hardly."

He regarded her with affection "How old, Lucy?"

"Twenty-three." She raised her eyebrows. "And you?"

"Twenty-six." He cracked a smile. "The perfect ages."

He heard a rumble from the street. "Mailman," Lucy said and watched as the man stopped and took something out of the mailbox before he drove on.

He felt her relax as the mailman drove away. "Do you want to go for a ride next week?" he asked.

She spun to face him. "Next week?"

"*Ja*, I have to spend some time in my workshop and making deliveries, but mostly, Jed King and some others are coming to work on my new store."

Lucy widened her eyes at his news. "You're going to open your own store! That's *wunderbor*, Gabriel!" She smiled.

He grinned. "'Tis something I've always wanted. I'm doing well, and while I haven't lived here long, I've made good contacts. I know what people—both Amish and English—like to buy. It will be easier for me to sell my merchandise in my own store, and I won't have to share the profits."

"Where will you build it?" she asked.

"Right on my property. Jed is going to help me convert part of the barn into the wooden crafts store." His eyes were full of excitement, and she loved seeing him this happy and pleased. "It will work best until I can move to a bigger space someday. The cost of renting isn't something I want to invest in right now. Maybe after my business expands enough for it to be an easy move."

Lucy nodded. "I understand. Someday when my children are grown, I may open my own bakery."

"You're doing well at King's and Peter's Pockets." He reached into his hand and pulled out a small sheet of paper, which he handed to her. "A few other shops who might be interested in selling your bakery items."

Lucy beamed at him. *"Danki,"* she breathed with an awed look in her pretty blue eyes. "Gabriel, I have a delivery to make in the morning, so I was wondering…" She bit her lip. "Would you hitch up my mare to my buggy?"

"You don't have to ask. I'll be by in the morning early and do it for you first thing."

Early the next morning, Gabriel returned to hitch Lucy's mare to her buggy. He grabbed the tack he'd need from inside the barn, then he went into the paddock with a chunk of apple that Lucy had given him to lure Blackie in. The mare was close to the outbuilding, so the apple worked well. As he held it out for the horse to eat, he grabbed onto her halter with his other hand. The mare munched happily and remained docile as he moved her from the paddock through a gate to the front of the buggy. Within a short time, Blackie was hitched to it, ready for Lucy to take later this morning.

Gabriel wished he could drive her where she needed to go, but he had things to do that could provide a better future for him…and anyone else he wanted to include in his life.

He got into Lucy's buggy and maneuvered it to where he could tie up the mare. He was finishing up when he sensed Lucy's presence. He turned and smiled at her. "You're all set."

"Danki." She regarded him warmly, and he felt her look clear down through him. She handed him a wrapped package. "Chocolate upside-down cake, a favorite of my brother-in-law and others within our community."

He smiled and touched her cheek. *"Danki*, Luce. I know I'll enjoy every bite." He wasn't ready to leave her, but he knew he had to go. "So next week? Will you and Susie take that ride with me?"

"Where are we going?"

"No place. Every place. Just for a ride to enjoy the sun and changing scenery. It will be the first week of summer. Will you come with me?"

"I'll come," she agreed. "What day?"

"Tuesday?"

She nodded, although she looked disappointed.

"Gut. Be ready early. By eight. I plan to make a day of it."

Her expression brightened. "We'll be ready."

Gabriel left, eager to see her again, but he had to

make sure he could provide for his future. And for the woman and two children he wanted in his life.

Tuesday seemed like a long way from now, Lucy thought as she and Susie got into her buggy that morning. She would take her daughter to Nancy's first. She would normally have Susie come with her, but this was the first time she'd driven since the accident, and she was nervous. It wasn't too far to Nancy's. Her sister-in-law, she knew, would be happy to keep Susie for the couple of hours she'd need to make her deliveries and do some shopping. Thankfully, her wrist was feeling much better, and she no longer needed to wear the Ace bandage at all.

Nancy was outside as Lucy pulled onto the lane that led to the Joseph Yost house. "*Hallo*, Lucy! Susie! What a lovely surprise!"

Lucy stepped down and waited until Susie climbed out after her. "I was hoping you wouldn't mind keeping Susie for a couple of hours. I have a few errands to run, and I think she'd enjoy being with you here more."

Nancy's smile was warm. "We'd love to have her. Susie, why don't you go inside? Sarah is in the kitchen eating breakfast. I made chocolate chip muffins this morning!"

Susie grinned. "Bye, *Mam*! See you later!" she cried and ran into the house.

After gazing after her for a few moments, Lucy met Nancy's eyes. *"Danki."*

"Are you *oll recht*?" Nancy asked, looking at her thoughtfully.

"*Ja*, I'm fine. Why?"

"I don't know. You seem off. Nervous."

Lucy gave her a wry smile. "My buggy just came out of the shop. It's been a while since I've used it."

But Nancy was shaking her head. "That's not it." She looked toward her buggy. "It looks brand-new."

"*Ja*. Eli Lapp did an amazing job fixing it." Lucy gasped. She should have kept silent.

"Did you have an accident in your buggy, Lucy?" Nancy walked over to Lucy's vehicle and examined it from all sides.

"Maybe a little one," Lucy admitted grudgingly.

She heard Nancy's sharp inhalation of breath, saw the concern on the woman's face. "What happened?"

"A car hit me from behind, spooking Blackie and sending my buggy into a ditch."

"Lucy!"

"I'm *oll recht*. I sprained my wrist, but it's fine now." Lucy bit her lower lip, debating. "That's how I met Gabriel. He stopped to help me."

"Praise the Lord for Gabriel." Nancy grew quiet. "How is he?"

"He's well, I think." Lucy wasn't ready to talk about her feelings for Gabriel Fisher. "I should get going. I won't be long. I need to deliver these cakes and pies."

"Are you coming over for Visiting Day?" Nancy asked.

"I…actually, Rachel King invited me to her and Jed's *haus*."

"*Gut*." Nancy grinned at her. "We've been invited, too. We'll drive you."

Relieved, Lucy smiled. "That would be nice. *Danki*. I should get going. I'll see you in a little while." She climbed into the driver's seat of her buggy and guided her horse around toward the road. She waved to her sister-in-law, who waved back but was gazing at her with worry. *I'll be fine*, she thought. *I'll always be fine no matter what happens in the future.*

She thought of Gabriel as she drove toward her first destination, Peter's Pockets, and felt happy. When she was done, she'd consult Gabriel's list and stop to talk briefly with the store owners.

It had been less than five hours since she'd seen Gabriel last, but she missed him all the same. Gabriel had business to take care of and so did she. Lucy concentrated on doing what needed to be done with the warmth and joy she felt in knowing that she'd be seeing him again in less than six days.

"I don't know, Gabriel," Jed King said as he examined the space Gabriel had selected for his store in the barn. "The existing walls aren't in the best shape. It might be better if you build a separate building. How big do you need it? Sixteen-by-sixteen?"

Gabriel frowned. He didn't want to hear that he couldn't use the barn, but Jed would know best, and if building his store there wasn't a good idea, he would listen to the former construction worker. "*Ja*, sixteen-by-sixteen would do."

"You could build it closer to the road for exposure. You own that strip of land on the other side of the barn?"

"*Ja*." Gabriel studied the land in question. "Why? You think the store should be built there?"

"I do. Why don't I work up a price for you for material, then you can let me know. There'll be no cost for labor, as you're one of us now." Jed grinned. "I'll ask Aaron Hostetler and a few others to help me. Aaron is particularly *gut* at this kind of work. With the group of us, it won't take but two days at the most to get it done."

Gabriel arched his eyebrows. "That fast?"

"*Ja.* 'Tis only sixteen feet. And don't you worry, we'll make it look inviting like any of the shops on Main Street. Will you need a stockroom?"

"No need for one. I'll keep extra stock in my workshop." Gabriel was excited. The prospect of the new store construction sounded wonderful. And it wouldn't take deep pockets to get it done.

Jed leaned against the picnic table in Gabriel's backyard and made a sketch of the building. "Something like this," he said as he showed it to Gabriel when he was done. "You can put a counter here. Have a window on each side wall for daylight. The front door will have glass in it and will give you more light. You can put shelves along here and here, and you may want glass in the counter where you can display your smaller wooden craft items."

Gabriel liked what he saw. "That looks *gut.* Let's do it!"

Jed gave him a smile that lit up his blue eyes. "It will feel *gut* to build something again." He paused. "I miss working in construction, but I do enjoy working in my family's store." He folded up the paper and placed it on the front seat of his vehicle. "Are you coming on Sunday? We're having friends over for Visiting Day. You and your sister are invited and most *willkomm.*"

"I appreciate that."

"I'll have the list of material and the cost ready for you."

"I'll see you then," Gabriel said as he stood back

while Jed climbed into his vehicle. "What can we bring?"

"Yourselves," Jed called out before he drove away.

Gabriel would have to ask Emily to make something. He wondered if he'd see Lucy there with Susie. He smiled at the prospect of seeing her sooner than their planned Tuesday outing.

Chapter Thirteen

Visiting Day at the Kings' was going to be a large event with friends and extended family. On Saturday morning, Lucy set about making two of the promised chocolate upside-down cakes that Nancy's family and others within their community had told her was their favorite dessert. Susie sat on the floor playing with her wooden waddling duck toy as Lucy measured the ingredients and set them in two separate bowls.

She was getting ready to mix up the first cake when she heard a car in the driveway. Curious, Lucy went to the door and stepped outside. She didn't recognize the car as belonging to one of her English neighbors. The rear door of the sedan opened and a tall man stepped out. He grabbed a satchel, paid the driver then watched as the car drove away. The man turned and Lucy gasped. It was her younger brother.

"Seth?" She ran toward the young man, who was actually a boy of thirteen, and skipped to a stop in front of him. *"Bruder?"*

Seth looked at her with dull eyes. "Lucy. *Vadder* told

me I had to come." He glanced down and saw her pregnant belly, and his bright blue eyes widened.

Lucy smiled. "*Willkomm!* I'm so glad to see you." She reached for his arm, gazing at him with warmth and love as she led him toward the house. She'd missed her brother and always wondered if he was happy with their father at home. "Come in!"

Susie appeared at the door. "*Mam?* Who's that?"

"That's my *bruder*—and your *onkel*." She climbed the two steps to the stoop and opened the door, pulling Seth inside the house with her. "His name is Seth."

Her daughter grinned. "*Hallo, Onkel* Seth. Are you going to live here now, too?"

Looking uncomfortable, Seth averted his gaze.

"*Ja*, he is," Lucy said, deciding immediately. "Isn't that *wunderbor*!"

Seth looked at her then with a glimmer of hope in his blue eyes so like her own.

"We've got lots of room *Onkel* Seth! Sit down. You must be hungry. Did you come from far away?" Susie asked. She turned to Lucy. "Where did he live before now, *Mam*?"

"Indiana, where I grew up."

Susie nodded and pulled out a chair for Seth, gesturing for him to sit. "I think you'll like it here better, *Onkel* Seth. We love it here. And you'll get to meet Gabriel. He's our friend. He can be your friend, too."

He took a seat silently. He hadn't said a word since he'd arrived, except to tell her that their father forced him to come. Lucy wondered—and worried—about what had happened to make Seth so quiet.

"*Mam*, can we give *Onkel* Seth some cake? *Mam* made a lemon cake yesterday. She bakes a lot," Susie said. "She bakes and sells her cakes and other things in stores. But she always makes some for us to keep. The cake has lemon frosting. Do you like lemon cake with lemon frosting?" Her daughter was talking like a chatterbox.

Seth gazed at Susie as the little girl talked, and Lucy caught the beginning of a smile on her younger brother's face.

Lucy couldn't believe that Seth was here. He was a teenager now, a young man. She hadn't seen him since he was nine years old, and he was the only person she missed since leaving their Amish community in Indiana.

"Seth," Lucy said softly. "*Danki* for coming. Our home is now yours."

He stared at her a long time, and she was shocked to see tears form in his eyes. "I... *Danki*," he whispered with gratitude, and Lucy smiled.

It was only later that she realized what Seth's arrival could mean for her and Gabriel. She had Susie and her baby on the way, and now she would be raising her thirteen-year-old brother. They'd never confessed their feelings in definite terms, although it had certainly been implied between them. Lucy sighed. Would Gabriel be willing to take on all of them as his family?

"Where's your husband?" Seth asked quietly that evening after dinner and Susie had left the room. Lucy was glad to see that her brother was now relaxed enough to feel comfortable. She'd cared for him after their mother had passed on, before her father had made her marry Harley and leave. She was overjoyed to have him here.

"*Dat* died," Susie said, having overheard, as she slipped back into the room. "A long time ago."

Seth's gaze locked with Lucy's. "Nearly six months ago now," she told him.

"I'm sorry," he said. "I didn't know. *Dat* didn't know."

"He didn't care," Lucy said without heat. "He's only concerned with Mari."

Her brother nodded. "I don't want to be a burden," he said.

"Seth, you could never be a burden. You're my *bruder*, and I love you. I've missed you. I was worried when you didn't write back to me."

"You wrote to me?" he asked, looking stunned.

"*Ja*, of course I did. I didn't want to leave you. When I didn't hear back, I wanted to visit, but Harley…was against it." She smiled to show him how happy she was that he'd come. "I can't believe how much you've grown."

Seth's lips twitched. "I don't remember you being this short. And I never expected to see that," he said with a gesture toward her baby belly. His expression sobered. "Are you happy about it?"

"About the *bubbel*? *Ja*," she replied with a soft smile. "I love Susie—she's my daughter, and I want nothing more than to give her a baby *bruder* or *schweschter*."

Susie climbed up onto her uncle's lap, shocking him. "I don't care what we have, do you? As long as our baby's healthy."

Seth took one long look into Susie's eyes and grinned. "'Tis a *gut* thing I'm here to help your *mam*, then, *ja*?" He tugged on her *kapp* string. "She's going to need all the help we can give her."

"Ja," Susie agreed. "You, me and Gabriel, too."

"Gabriel?" her brother asked.

"Our neighbor."

"And *Mam*'s *gut* friend. We love him," Susie said, making Lucy blush.

Seth suddenly looked worried. "I don't want to intrude."

"You're family, Seth. You belong with us." Lucy could never turn Seth away. If Gabriel didn't like it, there was nothing she'd be able to do about it.

Lucy sent up a silent prayer that Gabriel would understand that if he wanted a relationship with her, then he would have to accept everyone who came with her. Her stomach burned at the thought that she could lose him, but there was nothing she could do to change her situation or her life.

Visiting Day turned out to be a large event on Jed and Rachel's property. Nancy and her family came for her and Susie—and with the added surprise of Seth— and brought them to join in the gathering. When they arrived, Joseph parked with the other buggies on the far side of the barn. Lucy noted there were ten buggies, if not more, as they drove up next to the one on the far end and got out. Caleb climbed out after his parents and helped Susie down, followed by Sarah, Seth and Lucy. Lucy and Seth each carried one of her requested chocolate upside-down cakes. As they entered the yard, Lucy looked around to see how many people she knew.

Rachel broke away from a group of women to meet them. "Lucy, you made your cakes!"

"Ja," Lucy said with a smile. "How are you, Rachel?"

"Fine. Fine. Nice gathering, *ja*?" Her gaze scanned

the yard as if taking in the sight of all her guests. Her attention settled on Seth. "Who's this?" She smiled. "Wait, I can tell. You're Lucy's *bruder*."

Seth blinked. "How did you know?"

"We have the same color eyes," Lucy said. Eyes they'd inherited from Emma Troyer Graber, their mother.

"Come and I'll introduce you around." Rachel waved for them to follow her.

Lucy felt Seth looking at her and smiled. "'Tis fine. They are *gut* people here."

She started to trail after Seth, who was following Rachel, when she spied Gabriel at the far end of the backyard. He and Rachel's husband, Jed, were deep in a discussion. To Lucy's shock, Aaron Hostetler and several others were part of the group. She couldn't help wondering what they were talking about.

Emily Fisher approached her with a smile. "Lucy."

"*Hallo*, Emily. 'Tis nice to see you again." Lucy had trouble keeping her gaze from straying toward Gabriel.

"Are you looking at my brother or Aaron?" There was tension in the girl's voice.

"Gabriel."

Emily smiled. "I thought…" She exhaled loudly. "Aaron and I were seeing each other but then he pulled away, and I thought it was because of you."

Lucy was horrified. *"Nay!"*

Gabriel's sister laughed. "I can see that."

Gabriel happened to glance in her direction at that moment. After murmuring something to the other men, he left them and quickly headed her way. His expression was soft, his eyes warm, until he stumbled and she saw him grimace. He slowed his pace until he finally reached her side. "*Hallo*, Lucy. I'm happy to see you here." A small smile hovered on his lips.

"Don't mind me. I'll find someone else to talk with," Emily said with a chuckle.

To Lucy's astonishment, Gabriel's face turned red. "Sorry, Em. It's just that I haven't seen her in forever."

Emily's expression softened. "I'll leave you to her company, then," she said softly and left them alone.

"How are you, Lucy?" Gabriel asked, his eyes warm and affectionate. "I've missed you."

"I saw you talking earnestly with Jed and Aaron and some other men. What is that all about?"

"My store. I was going to convert part of my barn into the store, but Jed convinced me that it wasn't the best idea. He drew up plans for me. He, Aaron and a group of men from our community are going to do the work. They assure me that it won't take more than two days."

"That's *wunderbor*, Gabriel," she replied, sincerely happy for him. She glanced past him to see her brother headed her way. "Gabriel, something has changed at home," she said urgently. "There's something I need to tell you."

"Lucy!" Seth said with a grin. "They love your cake. They want to eat it before the meal!"

Lucy laughed. "Tell them to wait or I won't bring any next time."

"*Oll recht.*" Her brother left her then to return to a group of young people near the food table.

She turned back to Gabriel with a smile that quickly died when she saw the expression on his face. "Gabriel?"

"Who is that?" he asked as he reached down to rub his thigh.

She looked at his hand, and he immediately stopped what he was doing. "The someone I need to talk with you about—"

"Who is he?" he asked, his expression taunt.

Lucy gaped at him. "He's my *bruder*," she breathed, hurt by his tone. "Gabriel, what's wrong? Aren't you feeling well?"

"I'm fine."

But he didn't look well to her. She'd seen how his features had contorted briefly with pain before he regained control of it. "You don't look fine."

"I said I'm fine. So, your *bruder* has come to live with you?" he asked.

"That won't make a difference, will it? For us?"

"Lucy…" he began then stopped, looked away.

"You changed your mind about me."

He didn't meet her gaze.

"Listen, Lucy, we have to talk." He looked pained, regretful. "But not here."

Drawing a deep breath, Lucy studied him. "Something *is* wrong."

"I'll come by your *haus* this evening."

"Nay, if you want to talk, we'll talk now." She had to know what was bothering him.

"Fine."

Lucy felt a terrible sense of impending loss as she followed him toward the front of the house and around to the other side where trees separated the view from the backyard and no one was within earshot.

He halted abruptly and turned to her with pain in

his expression. "Lucy, I know we thought there was a possibility of a future with you but..."

"You've changed your mind."

"Ja." He looked away as if it was too painful for him to see her humiliation.

"Because of Seth—"

Gabriel stared at her then. "I have my reasons."

"Which doesn't mean *nay.*"

"I'm sorry."

She spun, eager to leave him. It hurt too much to spend time in the company she cared for too deeply to ever get over him. Without glancing back, she hurried away but then something made her stop when she was several yards away. What she saw made her inhale sharply. Gabriel was hunched over, staring at the ground while he rubbed his thigh. He looked so dejected that her heart thumped hard. But then his head lifted and he locked gazes with her. His hard stare made her realize that she'd been mistaken. She walked away, knowing that she'd left a huge chunk of her heart behind with Gabriel Fisher.

Since she had come with Nancy, she'd have to stay and keep her distance from Gabriel. She was falling for him, and she'd been so sure he had feelings for her too.

Lucy recalled the look in his eyes when he'd seen her across the yard and immediately broken away from the men to meet her. He'd seemed happy to see her. Gabriel had appeared ready to accept her and her two children, but adding a teenage boy into the mix had been too much for him and he'd ended their relationship.

He didn't once look at her at all as he rejoined the men's discussion in the yard. Needing time alone to think, she started to walk in another direction. She didn't want anyone to see her cry.

"What's wrong?" Emily Fisher asked from behind her.

Lucy froze then faced her, unable to control her tears. "'Tis nothing." She wiped a hand under each eye to wipe away the moisture.

The girl looked beyond her to where Gabriel was probably standing. Lucy didn't know for sure. "Gabriel," she said with a *tsk*. "Did you two argue?"

"Not exactly."

Seth came up to her and Emily then. "Hey, Lucy, some of the others want me to join in their baseball game. Is it *oll recht*?"

Lucy managed to control her hurt feelings to give her brother a genuine smile. "Of course. Have fun."

"Who's that?" Emily asked.

"Seth. My *bruder*."

Gabriel's sister stared a moment in the other direction and laughed. "Lucy, he's jealous! Of Seth!"

"*Nay*, Gabriel knows he's my *bruder*. I told him." Lucy continued to wipe her cheeks, making sure there was no lingering trace of her tears.

Emily narrowed her gaze. "I wonder what's bothering him. Maybe 'Tis his leg."

Lucy shook her head. "He said we needed to talk We did, and he broke up with me." *As if we were a couple instead of friends, although we were heading to become more.*

"He didn't!" The young woman was stunned.

"*Ja*, and I think I know why. 'Tis because Seth will be living with me now. I come with a young *dochter*, a *bubbel* on the way and now a thirteen-year-old boy. Too much for any man."

"*Nay*, Lucy. I don't think that's a problem for him. You mean something to my *bruder*, and no woman has meant anything to him since the fire. I could tell by the way he talks about you that you are someone special to him, more so than Lizzy, his former betrothed, ever was."

"Lizzy… I got the feeling that she hurt him badly," Lucy said.

"She devastated him," Emily explained, "breaking off their betrothal when he was at his most vulnerable. He was injured and needed her support but she only cared that he was a broken man who could no longer take care of her."

A tingle along the back of her neck made Lucy turn to find Gabriel staring at her, but when he saw her glance he turned quickly away. "Our friendship is new, and while I'd hoped we'd become more than friends, Gabriel doesn't want the same thing. I don't think he's ready for an instant family, and I understand. I really do, but I love Susie and Seth, and I already love my unborn baby."

"And Gabriel?" Emily asked, her expression serious, her voice quiet.

"I'll always care about Gabriel, Emily, but I know that he deserves better than all this responsibility."

"And what about me? Am I a complication you don't need?"

"*Nay*, Emily! You would always be a part of our family." Lucy clapped a hand over her mouth. "Oh."

Emily's expression softened. "Lucy, Gabriel has always wanted a family. Do you think having four new people in his life won't make him happy?" Emily shook her head. "If you think that, then you're wrong. He loves you but he's afraid. He wants you but feels he is too damaged to have you."

Lucy shook her head. "He's not the damaged one. I am," she said.

"He's the one who suffered the loss of his family. He's the one with the scarred leg," Emily pointed out. "Not you."

She knew Emily was right, but she still kept away from him. She remembered how he'd rubbed his thigh until she caught him at it. Had he been in pain? What that why he'd pushed her away? It didn't matter, she decided. She wanted to leave but she couldn't ask her sister-in-law to go. While Lucy felt miserable, Nancy and her family were having a wonderful time.

She ate and engaged in conversation with her new friends Rachel, Maggie and Hannah. If they noticed that she was sad, they didn't comment. Lucy hoped they couldn't tell how bad she felt inside.

At least twice, she saw Gabriel head in her direction, and she fled to avoid him, pretending an eagerness to join in a conversation with a group of women.

Finally, people began to leave. Lucy, more than ready, waited with Susie and Seth near the buggy for Nancy and the rest of her family to come and take them home.

She could feel Gabriel's gaze on her but she refused to acknowledge him.

Minutes later, she was headed home and couldn't be more relieved to reach the privacy of her small house.

"I'll see you soon," Nancy called out after Joseph had dropped off her family, before they'd left.

"Lucy?" Seth asked as she climbed the steps and unlocked the door. "Are you *oll recht*?"

Lucy managed a smile for him. "I'm fine. Does anyone want a snack and a drink? I have some homemade chocolate chip cookies!" she said cheerfully, although she didn't feel happy.

"*Ja, Mam!* Seth, can you get *Mam*'s cookie tin! I'd like milk with my cookies. What about you, Seth?"

Lucy heard Seth tease her daughter, and she finally managed a genuine smile. She might have lost Gabriel but she still had Seth, Susie and her unborn baby. She'd somehow find comfort in her little family.

Gabriel was tense as he and his sister drove home from the Kings'.

"You are an idiot," Emily said.

He glared at her. "Excuse me?" His thigh ached something terrible and he stifled the urge to rub it. It had started to cramp up when he'd approached Lucy. In fact, it had hurt so bad he'd nearly stumbled and fell. Right then and there, he should have turned around and stayed away from her. It wasn't good for a man to snap at the woman he was falling in love with. But loving her didn't change the fact that he was too much of a damaged man to be good for her.

"You love Lucy yet you're ready to give up your relationship with her." She shook her head. "You're a fool, Gabriel Fisher. I thought you were a smart man, but you're not."

The truth of her words hit him hard. He hadn't told her how the stabbing pain had returned frequently and that he'd been hiding it so that she wouldn't worry. He hadn't confided in her about the surgery he might have to undergo that might help with the pain. He still had other options, but he feared that none of them would work. He still wasn't sure he could ever agree to another operation, but he might not have any choice. "Emily, you don't understand—"

"I understand that you are too willing to give up a chance at happiness with the woman you love. Lucy is *gut* for you, Gabriel. I've never seen you this happy before."

Gabriel stayed silent. He didn't know what to say. "I'm broken, Em."

"Broken? What, physically?" Emily said. "*Nay!* Broken inside, maybe. How do you think Lucy feels? She has a father who doesn't love her enough to keep her at home. *Nay*, he had to marry her off to get rid of her so he could wed a pretty young wife. Then she had a husband who gave her a sweet daughter, but did he care for her? Love her? *Nay*." She placed her hand on his arm to draw his attention. "I don't know what is going through that thick head of yours, but you need to think long and hard about your relationship with her."

"I have been." And he'd done the right thing—the best thing—for Lucy.

He'd thought he'd gotten over the worst of the pain. He'd lived a couple of days pain free since he'd seen the doctor. And then the pain had returned, its intensity worse than before. Maybe he should see Dr. Jorgensen again, he thought. Did he really want to lose Lucy forever? No, he didn't. Maybe he needed to find out more about the surgery he eventually could be forced to have.

Gabriel said in a strangled voice. "My leg's been bad, Em. Really bad. Nothing seems to be helping."

"*Ach nay, bruder.*"

He closed his eyes. "I can't be a burden to her."

She studied him with sympathy. "She cares about you, too, you know."

"What if she no longer does because she's tired of having to deal with me as I am?" He faced her, feeling vulnerable. "My leg, Em. The doctors said that if nothing else works, I might need surgery."

"Oh, Gabriel…" Emily said softly. "You can't let your leg rule your life. Lucy isn't Lizzy. She's a better person. She's strong and the right woman for you. She will understand that you'll have *gut* and bad days. All you have to do is explain and convince her you love her and want her in your life."

He huffed out a laugh. "That's all?"

Emily snickered. "*Bruder,* I didn't say it would be easy."

Chapter Fourteen

Gabriel had messed up with Lucy. He loved her desperately, but because of his fears and unwillingness to share all of his pain with her, he had hurt her badly. His sister was right, he knew. Lucy had become important to him, and he'd driven her away before she could leave him. His leg had been hurting, but that was no excuse. It was possible that it would always hurt him. He couldn't let it stop him, not if he wanted to live again. Perhaps she would forgive him after he explained. But what if he needed the surgery? He didn't want to put Lucy through the worry of the procedure and his recovery afterward. He realized with sudden clarity that he'd been afraid she would leave him like Lizzy had. But as Emily reminded him, Lucy wasn't Lizzy. Lizzy had been weak, while Lucy was strong. He had never loved Lizzy the way he loved Lucy. He gasped. *Ja*, he loved Lucy! He couldn't give her up, but would he be able to convince her to give him another chance.

Lucy Schwartz was a loving, wonderful mother and a sweet woman, and he could easily envision her as his wife and the mother of his children. He wanted Susie and her baby for his own, and Seth... He would enjoy raising Lucy's brother. The boy needed a man who cared about him, who would stand by him and teach him things that a man needed to know.

He realized he'd never gotten over the trauma of the fire, the loss of his family compounded by the rejection from the woman he'd thought he'd loved. He should have gotten help, but instead he'd suffered in silence, and had been afraid and acted foolishly because he hadn't been able to get past what had happened to his family, to Emily. To him.

He should have spoken openly with her about his feelings. That would have done more for him than any doctor ever could.

Lucy meant more to him than Lizzy ever had. Would he be able to fix things with her? Would she ever forgive him for being *doom-kop*?

Before Visiting Day, Lucy had agreed to go for a ride with him on Tuesday. He would visit her then and convince her to go on that ride. But first, he needed to talk with Seth. What if the boy didn't want him in his life? He understood that Seth would come first. Gabriel wanted her even if he would always be last. He loved her that much. And Seth? If Seth was all right having him as part of the family, then he would ask for the boy's help.

Gabriel left the house for the new store building that Jed, Aaron and two other men were building for him. He liked Jed, but he didn't know how he felt about Aaron. His sister had liked him, but he'd disappointed her because of Lucy—although Lucy had told him that she didn't want the man in her life. He'd believed her. He still did.

He should trust her. He *did* trust her. He was his own

worst enemy, and he knew it. He had to change, or else lose all chance of happiness with the woman he had fallen in love with.

It was Tuesday morning, and his store building was nearly done, with windows and two doors. Jed and Eli Brubaker were whitewashing the exterior walls. Gabriel heard hammering inside and wondered what Aaron and Matthew Bontrager were doing.

"Looks *gut*," he said after he'd greeted Jed.

Jed stopped what he was doing to smile at him. "Told you it wouldn't take us long. We started it on Friday and we'll be done with it by the end of today. Aaron and Matt are inside working on your counter and your shelves." He paused. "What color do you want your door and trim? Something other than white, *ja*?"

"What do you think?"

"How about blue?"

Gabriel nodded. "Sounds *gut*. I'll let you pick the color." He stood back and gazed at the building with a good feeling. "May I look inside?" he asked.

"'Tis your place," Jed said, brushing on another swipe of white paint. "Go on in."

He opened the door and spied Aaron without a hat, his blond hair damp with sweat as he worked on the store counter. Three sides had been nailed together, leaving an opening in the front. The Formica top for the counter was leaning against the far wall. "What's that for?" Gabriel asked, gesturing toward the open end.

"For glass or plexiglass or whatever you want to put there to create a display case." Aaron barely looked him in the eyes. The man was clearly uncomfortable after learning that Emily was Gabriel's sister.

"Where's Matt?"

"He went out to pick up some wood screws and brackets for the shelves. We thought we had enough but we don't."

Gabriel chewed the inside of his mouth as he watched the other man work on his knees, checking measurements and driving nails in deep to hold the counter together. "Are you in love with Lucy?" he asked Aaron.

"What? *Nay!* She was my best friend's wife. I was worried about her."

"You don't need to be. I'll take care of Lucy from now on if she'll let me. I messed up with her but I intend to fix it."

Aaron glanced up at him with surprise. "You know Lucy?" His face lit up as the truth dawned on him. He smiled. "You know Lucy," he said softly. "Well, now I understand." He put down his hammer and stood, wiped the dampness from his brow. "Does she feel the same way?"

"I thought so, but I'm not sure," Gabriel admitted.

"I wish you all the best," Aaron said, sounding sincere. "Lucy tries to be independent."

"I know she does." He smiled. "And I like that about her, as long as she still allows me to help her." Gabriel needed to know what the man thought of his sister. "What about Emily? How do you feel about her?" He paused. "She's my sister."

The man's expression softened. "I like her."

"You canceled supper," Gabriel pointed out.

"Got hurt on the job that afternoon. Was in the emergency room."

"Why didn't you tell her?"

He crouched down to pick up his hammer. "My *bruder* was supposed to tell her."

"He didn't. He just told her that you weren't coming."

Aaron scowled. "No wonder she won't talk to me." Setting down his hammer, he rose to his feet. "I'll need to have a talk with her. I won't leave until she listens to me."

Gabriel chuckled. "I wish you all the best in that. Emily tends to be independent, like Lucy."

The other man cracked a smile. "That's what we love about them, *ja*?"

"Absolutely." He looked around the interior of the store, pleased with how it was shaping up. "This will work perfectly. *Danki* for taking the job with Jed and the others."

With a nod and a smile, Aaron bent down to get his hammer. "We'll be done today."

"So I hear. I appreciate it." Gabriel left the store and went to his workshop. Last night, he'd worked long into the night on something special for Lucy. She might not want it, but he'd put his heart and soul…and love…into this gift for her. He'd stained and varnished it last night, and he knew it was ready.

The cradle was well constructed, sanded smooth and stained, and it was just the right size for a newborn to use until he or she was several months old. Gabriel had debated whether or not to paint a design on the sides but then decided not to, not without Lucy's permission. Besides, he had no idea if she was carrying a boy or a girl.

He could use the cradle as an excuse to see her, but he didn't think it was right to do that. Besides, he wanted to talk with her brother, Seth, first, explain what he wanted—a life with Lucy, Susie, the baby and Seth. Would the boy accept him into his life? Would Lucy decide he wasn't worth a second chance with her time, her friendship...or her love?

Gabriel left the workshop and let his sister know that he was going out, before he got into his buggy to make the drive down the road to Lucy's house. If he could find Seth alone outside, he might be able to initiate a man-to-man talk with him. If he could make Seth understand how he felt, then maybe, with the boy's help, he'd have a chance at forever with the woman he loved.

Despite that he'd long given up the hope of a forever life with any woman before he met Lucy, he didn't want to live without her. He needed her and she needed him, but mostly he loved her and he thought she returned his love. If she did, maybe he'd have his forever after all.

He'd start with Seth and then go from there, for if the teenager didn't want him in Lucy's life, then Lucy wouldn't want him either. But he prayed that wouldn't be the case.

Tuesday morning Lucy felt listless. She was tired. She hadn't slept well since Sunday, after she and Gabriel had had words. He'd hurt her, and she'd become angry. Anger was a sin, and she felt terrible about it, repentant. She'd prayed to the Lord since he'd discarded her friendship. She still didn't have an idea of what the Lord had decided where she and Gabriel were concerned.

She missed him. With every breath she took, she missed him, and she wished they could redo Visiting Day and that things had gone differently. She should have asked about his leg, pushed to know the truth of why he had rejected her.

The more Lucy thought about that moment, the more she realized that there was more Gabriel hadn't told her. That he hadn't been scared off by the prospect of a ready-made family.

Gabriel has always wanted a family, Emily had said. *Do you think having four new people in his life won't make him happy? If you do, then you're wrong. He loves you but he's afraid. He wants you but feels he is too damaged to have you.*

And she had told Emily that she was the damaged one. She recalled Gabriel's concern with how people would react to him. She hated that he often felt that way. He was an attractive man who just happened to have a burn scar on his left cheek.

He had a severe one on his leg, too. Gabriel had admitted as much and said he wasn't ready to show it to her. Was it because he was afraid that she wouldn't want him, love him, if she saw it? And exactly how much did it bother him?

"Oh, Gabriel," she whispered. "Don't you know there is nothing that will ever make me stop loving you?"

How was she going to fix this? Should she go to his house to talk with him? It had only been one day. Maybe she should wait another day or two to give him time for clarity. Then she would approach him for a calm discussion during which she'd demand to know the truth, because the more she thought about it, the more she realized that he hadn't explained why he thought they should stop seeing each other.

Lucy tried to keep busy, and her baking helped to keep her mind occupied. Still, thoughts of Gabriel lingered. As she made a chocolate cake, she remembered how much he loved her chocolate cream pie. When she made lemon squares, she recalled the first time she'd met Emily. Every ingredient she picked reminded her of Gabriel in some way. When she finished her baking, she gazed at the vast number of sweets that covered her countertop and kitchen table. And still thought about Gabriel as she looked at them.

She laughed without humor. It wasn't the ingredients, nor was it her cakes and pies that made her think of Gabriel. It was the fact that her love for him was lodged so deeply inside of her that she couldn't let it go. She didn't want to let it go. She'd never let it go.

The door behind her opened and slammed shut as Seth entered the house. "Lucy, do you need any help with anything?"

"You've driven a buggy before, *ja*?"

"I'm thirteen years old, not three, *schweschter*," he said with a teasing roll of his eyes. "Of course I have."

Lucy nodded. "If I give you a list, would you pick up a few things at the store for me?"

"*Ja*, I'll be happy to go for you."

"Where's Susie?" she asked as she jotted down several items with a pencil on paper.

Seth moved to peek out the window. "She's outside in the yard. Do you want me to take her with me?"

"*Nay*, I'd like her to come inside and rest for a while." Lucy felt terrible, for she'd sensed that Susie noticed a change in Lucy's relationship with Gabriel. Like Lucy, her daughter had slept badly ever since.

Seth took the list Lucy handed him, looked it over. "Where can I find these things?" he asked.

"King's General Store. Just make a left from our property and continue straight until you see the store on your right. Think you can find the way?"

Her brother nodded. "I'll get Susie for you before I go."

Lucy smiled and touched her brother's cheek. "*Danki*, Seth. Have I told you how much I love having you here?"

Seth smiled. "I never get tired of hearing it. And you should know that I love living here with you." Her brother exited the house and returned within minutes with Susie. "Here she is."

"You wanted me, *Mam*?"

"*Ja, dochter.* I'd like you to lie down with me. Will you do that?"

Susie tilted her head as she met Lucy's gaze. "With you?"

"*Ja.*"

"*Oll recht.*"

Seth hadn't left yet. "We're going to take a nap," Lucy told him. "Would you mind putting away the groceries for me after you bring them home?" Her brother nodded and left, and Lucy headed wearily upstairs with Susie, where they both lay down on her bed and rested. Her new resolve to talk with Gabriel again eased her mind a little, allowing her to fall asleep.

As he neared Lucy's property, Gabriel saw her buggy leave her driveway. He realized immediately that it wasn't Lucy who was driving. It was Seth. Recognizing a good opportunity when he saw one, he followed the vehicle until it turned into the parking lot of King's General Store and pulled all the way around to the hitching post in the back instead of using the one on the side of the building. He pulled in and parked beside Lucy's buggy, got out and tied up his horse as Seth secured Blackie.

Gabriel circled his vehicle. "Seth."

The teenager stiffened as he turned. He was tall for his age, an attractive boy with dark hair like his sister, and he also had Lucy's bright blue eyes. He wore a royal blue shirt and black tri-blend pants held up with black suspenders. His black-banded straw hat had a smaller brim than Gabriel's. "How do you know my name?"

"My name is Gabriel Fisher," he introduced himself pleasantly. "I live down the road from your sister."

Seth stared at him, narrowed his eyes. "You're Lucy and Susie's friend."

"Actually, Lucy and I had a bit of a disagreement, which I'd like to talk about, if you'll let me."

The boy looked uncertain. "I don't know." He glanced around the parking lot to see if anyone was watching them. "I'm not sure that Lucy would want me to."

Gabriel inhaled and went for it. "Seth, I love your sister. I want to marry her and I want you, Susie and the baby to be my family. Will you help me? I messed up and I could really use your help."

Seth blinked. "You want to marry my sister?"

Relieved that Seth didn't appear to be against the idea, Gabriel nodded. "*Ja.* But I... I need to talk with her, and I would like to talk with her alone. Do you think you could take Susie over to see her cousins, Sarah and Caleb, tomorrow morning? About nine? Last week Lucy agreed to go for a ride with me today, but..."

Seth cracked a smile. "I get it. I'll help, if you're sure this is what you want." His smile disappeared. "I don't want Lucy hurt. My *vadder* hurt her enough to last a lifetime."

And hurt you as well, Gabriel thought, recognizing pain when he saw it in the boy's eyes. "I have never been more sure of anything in my life." He bucked up for what he had to say next. "And if she doesn't want me to be in her life, I'll respect that. The last thing I want to do is hurt or bother her." He shifted from one foot to the other. "What do you say?"

The boy grinned. "I'd say *willkomm* to the family, but you'll have to convince her of that first, *ja*?"

Gabriel laughed at the boy's teasing. "*Ja*. What are my chances?"

Seth tilted his head while he seemed to give it some thought. *"Gut,"* he said. "More than *gut*, I think."

He saw the list in the boy's hand "Do you need a hand with shopping?"

Lucy's brother looked at his list. "*Nay*, 'tis a short list."

"Don't always expect it to be so with your sister, Seth," Gabriel said as he headed toward his buggy and was gratified to hear the boy laugh.

The next morning, Gabriel was up and dressed early while it was still dark. To say he was nervous was putting it lightly. His future with Lucy depended on his apology and his convincing her to give him a second chance. They'd never talked about a future together, but he'd certainly thought about one from the first moment he'd laid eyes on her. He'd denied it, but he knew it was true. He had an ugly burn scar and persistent trouble with his leg. Would Lucy really want a man who was that damaged? He'd have to explain that eventually he might have to undergo surgery. He would upfront and honest. He prayed that it would be enough to win her love.

Then he thought about his feelings for Lucy, how

Susie, her unborn child and now the newest member of her family, Seth, hadn't changed his love for her. Her family members only enhanced his love. She was everything he'd ever wanted in a woman. He could see them years from now, working side by side in the house, in their store. His new store might not be big enough for Lucy's bakery items, but it would do until they found a bigger place, a bigger house, for he wanted more children with Lucy.

At eight forty-five, Gabriel put the cradle he'd made for Lucy's baby into the back of his buggy then headed toward Lucy's house. If she rejected him, he'd leave the cradle and go. He wanted her to have it. He'd planned to give her something special, and the baby cradle seemed like a good thing for an expectant mother. And if she accepted him into her life, then the cradle would hopefully get a lot of use, he thought with a smile.

He saw Seth leaving the property with Susie, the boy driving the buggy with expert hands. Seth was going to make a fine man, he thought. And if he had anything to do with it, Seth would never doubt that he was loved and wanted in his sister's home—which would hopefully be his, too.

When the buggy was but a spot in the distance, Gabriel turned onto Lucy's property and parked close to the road. He hoped that Lucy hadn't heard him arrive. He wanted to surprise her, catch her off guard. He left the cradle in the buggy and walked the rest of the way toward the house. His leg tightened up, but he breathed through it. He wasn't going to allow his pain to keep him from the woman he loved—this new feeling was also giving him a new determination.

He continued until he reached the top of her stoop and knocked.

"What did you forget, Seth?" he heard Lucy say as the door opened. She gaped at him. "Gabriel!"

"*Hallo*, Lucy," he ventured shyly. "May I come in?"

She wouldn't look away. "*Ja.*" She stepped aside as he entered.

He pulled off his hat and hung it up as he usually did on the wall hook. "Yesterday, we had plans for a ride."

Lucy frowned. "I thought they were canceled."

"I understand why you thought that," he acknowledged with a nod. "May I tell you something?"

Lucy's blue eyes filled with wariness. "What is it?"

"I love you. I'm sorry for the way I acted. I love you so much and I want to marry you, if you'll have me." He held up his hand and rushed on when she opened her mouth to speak. "I want you and Susie and your baby…and Seth. I want all of you to be my family. I'm not an easy person to live with. I can be irritable when my leg hurts. And, Lucy, my leg…it's ugly. It's ugly and sometimes I feel terrible stabbing pains while other times I feel pins and needles. I've seen my neurologist, Dr. Jorgensen, and he's working with me to help with the pain. And the pain gets bad sometimes. I may need surgery if my doctor doesn't find another way to manage it. I didn't want to put you through the worry, but I can't live without you. You don't deserve someone as damaged as me, but I'm asking for a second chance anyway. I've never met anyone like you. I've never loved anyone as much as you." He closed his eyes in silent prayer before he continued. "Be my wife, my love, and the mother of not only the children we have already but our future children. We can own a store together. We'll sell my wooden crafts and your cakes and pies. I don't expect an answer right away," he said. "I'll give you all the time you need, but please give me a chance at loving you…at loving our ready-made family."

He turned, picked up his hat and reached for the door.

"Where do you think you're going?" Lucy said softly.

Gabriel turned, faced her. The light in her blue eyes and the softness in her expression gave him hope. "Lucy?"

"*Ja*, Gabriel. I will marry you. I decided I'd never marry again unless it was for love. And I do love you, Gabriel." Tears filled her eyes as she gazed at him. "Just do me a favor? Talk to me when something bothers you so we work things out when there is a problem, and I promise to do the same."

He eyed her with joy. "I promise," he said as he hung up his hat again. He went to her, pulled her into his arms and kissed her on the forehead. "I love you, Lucy."

"I love you, Gabriel."

"And now we wait until Seth gets home with Susie so we can tell them both."

Lucy frowned. "How did you know that Seth left with Susie?"

His lips twitched. "I may have had a little help so that I could get a few minutes alone with you to apologize and propose."

"You talked with Seth?" she asked with raised eyebrows.

"I did, and he is *oll recht* with it, as long as this is something you want."

Lucy grinned and leaned her head against his chest, and he instinctively tightened his arms around her.

Gabriel pulled back to look her in the eyes. "Lucy, I

want you to see my leg before we wed. It's not a pretty sight, and I'll understand if you want to change your mind."

"*Nay.*"

"*Nay?*" He gazed at her in shock. "You don't want to see it?"

"*Nay*, I'll never change my mind. I love who you are and everything about you, including your left leg."

"Wait here, then."

"Gabriel—"

"I'll be right back, Lucy."

He went outside to his buggy, which he drove closer to the house. He tied up his horse then reached into the back of the vehicle to pull out something long, wooden and familiar.

She gasped as he brought it into the house.

"I wanted to make you something special," he said as he set it down.

"Gabriel, 'tis beautiful." She bent down to touch it, running her fingers over the smooth, polished wood. When she straightened, she had tears in her eyes. "I love it. I love you. *Danki.*"

They sat at the kitchen table eating pie and making plans while they waited for Seth and Susie to come home. A little while later, Gabriel insisted on showing her his leg, and he rolled up his pants leg as far as it would go so she'd get a hint of what lay underneath it.

"You can't see the worst of it," he told her, watching her closely.

She smiled. "I don't care. I love you, and that's all that matters." She seemed unaffected by the scarred tissue, the discoloration. "And, Gabriel, if you need surgery, I'll be there for you. We'll get through it together. All of us as a family, because that's what we do when we love each other."

"Lucy," he whispered, his expression filled with love.

"You've nothing to worry about," she assured him.

"I have other scars, too. They had to harvest some of my own skin for grafting. I'm a scarred, broken man. Are you sure you're ready to take me on? For all of it?"

"I'm positive." Lucy gazed at the man across from her and her heart melted. She loved him so much. Her baby moved, and the flutter made her smile. In two months, she and Gabriel would welcome a baby son or daughter.

"I'd like to get married soon, if that is *oll recht* with you," Gabriel said, his gaze settling on her belly where her hand lay.

"How soon?" She shifted in her chair.

"I thought as soon as I get permission from the church elders. I'll talk with the bishop after I leave here. We don't have to wait until November since you're a widow. But we will have to wait for the banns to be read."

"So next month?" Lucy asked with a smile.

"*Ja*, that's what I was thinking."

She nodded. "I like that idea." She grew thoughtful. "Where will we live?"

"We can live here if you'd like until we can buy a bigger place. The store is on my property but that's only a half mile from here, an easy commute. The counter will have a glass case in it, Lucy. The others thought it would be good place to feature small items and toys, but I think it will be a great place to sell your cookies and cakes."

Lucy smiled. "I like that idea—"

The side door slammed open, and Susie ran inside first. "Gabriel!"

"*Hallo*, little one."

"You didn't come before now," she said with a frown.

He nodded gravely. "*Ja*, I know, little one, but that's going to change."

Seth entered moments later. He looked first to Gabriel then to her. "Lucy?"

"*Ja*, Seth. We're going to be a family."

Susie gazed at the two of them and frowned. "Who is going to be a family?"

"You, Seth, the baby, and Gabriel and me. Gabriel and I are going to get married. Is that *oll recht* with you?"

"*Ja!*" Her daughter jumped up and down in her excitement. "We love him, and we want him to be our family."

Lucy laughed. "*Ja*, we do." Her gaze went to her brother, who remained awfully quiet. "Seth? Are you *oll recht* with having Gabriel in our lives?"

He nodded. "Are you sure you want me?"

Gabriel rose, went to Seth and grabbed hold of the boy's shoulders. "Seth, you belong here, more than I do, but I'd like to be part of your family, if you'll let me."

"*Ja?*" Lucy was surprised to see Seth blink back tears. Her eyes welled up with her own as she watched the man she loved reassure her brother.

"*Ja*," Gabriel said, squeezing Seth's shoulders lightly before releasing him. He turned toward Susie. "Susie?"

With a cry of joy, Susie flew into his arms and hugged him hard. Lucy saw him wince slightly where her daughter grabbed him but his expression never changed. "I love you, Gabriel," her child said.

He settled his hand on her head affectionately. "I love you, too, little one."

Epilogue

Winter, New Berne,
A year and a half later

"Gabriel."

Lucy's voice nudged him awake. He must have fallen asleep. They had been relaxing in upholstered armchairs side by side in their great room. Gabriel opened his eyes and smiled at his wife. They were married well over a year now, having wed six weeks from the day they'd first met. He loved every moment of their life together. Their family was like a never-ending adventure with excitement and love. Being her husband and a father, he was the happiest he'd ever been. He stretched and shifted in the chair. His leg was stiff, but the new medication his doctor had put him on was working. Surgery might be an option for the future but for now his leg had improved without it.

Gabriel reached out to run a finger across Lucy's cheek. "I must have dozed off."

"Me, too," she said with warmth in her pretty blue eyes.

They had been sharing a quiet moment together this

afternoon. Susie and Jacob were spending the night with Rachel and Jed King. Nancy had offered to take them, but Susie wanted to spend time with her new friend Bess, Rachel's daughter. Rachel was also good with their son Jacob, a toddler who needed a younger woman like her to take care of him. The Jed Kings had become a close friends with him and Lucy, and he was grateful for the couple they trusted with their children.

Worried because his sister's time was near, Seth was outside, shoveling snow off the walkway and driveway. He had been a big help with Susie and Jacob, always lending a hand, keeping an eye on both children. He also helped out in the store whenever Gabriel needed him. Seth had gone with the children to the Kings' in the hired car earlier before the driver had brought him back to the property where the boy had immediately started to work.

Gabriel thought highly of the boy. Seth had finished eighth grade, his last year of school, and he was happy, healthy and glad to be a part of their family.

They'd had one terrible day when Lucy had received a second letter from her father, requesting Seth's return. Seth was happy here and had refused to go. Lucy had written her father back to tell him. That was six months ago, and they hadn't heard a word from the man since. If he wrote again, he and Lucy would handle his demands together. Seth belonged to them, and no one, especially not his own father, would take him away or make him feel less than he was ever again.

He and Lucy were enjoying these rare peaceful moments together that didn't come often with two young, energetic children—and with their third to arrive any day now—in the household. With the blustery, wintry weather outside, Gabriel had closed Fishers' Store, their successful toys and treats shop in the building on his old property that now belonged to his sister Emily. No one would be venturing outside on a day like today, and he was glad, for he loved spending this quality time with his Lucy.

The snowfall blanketing the ground made the countryside beautiful. It was the perfect day to spend inside with his beloved wife in their new home. They had sold Lucy's house and bought another one large enough for their growing family, property with a paved driveway and sidewalk. Emily was living in their old house, and she was seeing someone new.

Gabriel gazed at his wife with a smile until he saw pain move across Lucy's features and he became immediately concerned. Alert now, he straightened. "What's wrong?"

"'Tis time."

"The baby?" He felt a little nervous flutter in his chest as he studied her.

She sat up, straightening her back, and groaned. *"Ja."* She rubbed her hands across her belly in its advanced stage of pregnancy. Apparently, their *bubbel* was ready to face the world.

Gabriel had planned for this time. If he hadn't, he would be more panicked than he already was at the thought of getting her to the hospital on snowy streets. "What do you need?"

A sound at the door heralded Seth as the boy entered the house. He stomped snow off his boots before he took them off. He pulled off his woolen hat, revealing a mop of unruly dark hair. He removed his jacket and gloves then grinned at them. The grin fell off his face when his gaze landed on his sister.

"Seth, here is my cell phone," Gabriel said. "Call the doctor by hitting number three and let her know we'll be heading to the hospital soon. Then if you'll dial for me, I'll call—"

"Bert," Seth finished for him, already grabbing the phone to make the first call.

Gabriel remained calm while Seth called Lucy's obstetrician and then Bert Hadden, their English friend who had stopped to help them after Lucy's accident. The man was waiting to spring into action and drive them to the hospital in his four-wheel-drive vehicle that easily handled the snow.

This wasn't the first time Gabriel had been with Lucy when she'd delivered a baby. While Seth remained with Susie at home, he'd waited anxiously in the waiting room when she'd gone into labor less than a month after they'd married. Finally allowed into his wife's hospital room after Lucy had endured a C-section, Gabriel had looked at the baby boy in his mother's arms and fallen instantly in love. Their son, Jacob, had his wife's blue eyes and her late husband Harley's blond hair. And soon she would give birth to a third child, the one they'd created together, a child they'd love like they did their other children. He was nervous but eager to meet the newest addition to their family.

Seth put the phone on speaker and handed it to Gabriel. "Hello?" Bert said.

"Bert! This is Gabriel," he said. "It's time."

"I'm on my way," the gruff man said and immediately hung up the phone. Gabriel grinned, knowing the man would get there in record time and that he would get them safely to the hospital on the increasingly snowy roads.

"Are you *oll recht*, Lucy?" Seth asked with concern. He hesitantly approached his sister.

"I'm fine, *bruder*, just having a baby," Lucy assured him with a grin, reaching up to give the boy's arm a squeeze, making Gabriel love her all the more.

With loving hands, Gabriel helped his wife to rise and bundled her into her heavy woolen coat. Lucy was a vision of loveliness with her bright eyes, big belly and the smile she reserved for him. The knock came minutes later, revealing Bert, who had left his vehicle idling and ready to go.

"Do you want to come?" Gabriel asked Seth.

The boy blinked. "You don't mind?"

"You're family. Come with us."

Seth shook his head. "I would, but I should make sure the *haus* stays warm."

Gabriel nodded in understanding.

Barely an hour later, Lucy gave birth to a daughter. Gabriel gazed through eyes filled with tears at their precious baby girl with her fine wispy dark hair the same color as his and Lucy's. He knew Susie was going to be so happy to finally have a sister.

"She's *wunderbor*," he told his wife. "Every day, every month and every hour, you never cease to amaze me. I love you, Lucy Fisher, and I love our baby girl. I never thought I'd ever be this happy."

"Gabriel," she whispered, "you have made me feel loved, and I'm so grateful to have you as my husband and the father of our *kinner. Gott* has surely blessed our marriage and our family. *Danki* for loving me…and our little ones. For loving Seth."

"I love you. I love our family, Luce, and with you by my side, I will love and guide our children for as long as we are on this earth together."

"Are you ready for life to get noisier and a bit wilder with a six-year-old, a one-year-old and a newborn?"

"*Ja*, I'll always be ready for life with you, dear wife." He grinned. "Besides, we have Seth. He's becoming a man."

Lucy smiled tiredly. Their daughter's birth had gone well, but she was still exhausted. "What shall we call our *dochter?*"

Gabriel leaned over to kiss his wife's cheek. "We could call her Miracle, for she, like Susie and Jacob, is a precious gift given to us by *Gott.*"

His wife shook her head but continued to smile. "Let's call her Grace."

He was infused with warmth, like he'd been kissed by the summer sun. "Our *bubbel dochter* came to us by the grace of *Gott.*" He blinked back tears. "I love that," he said. "I love you." He leaned down and kissed her sweetly.

"I love you, Gabriel," Lucy replied. "You and our family."

"Not as much as I love you." He grinned and she laughed. Life was good.

* * * * *

Dear Reader,

Welcome to New Berne in Lancaster County, Pennsylvania, home of Lucy Schwartz and Gabriel Fisher and all of the other wonderful Amish folks who live there!

The Amish settlement is an hour north by buggy to Happiness, the setting for many of my other books. Lucy is a young, pregnant widow with a four-year-old daughter. She wasn't in love with her late husband, and so she doesn't want another man in her life and is happy to raise her daughter and the child she will soon have on her own. But then she meets Gabriel Fisher, a woodworker and toy maker who was wounded badly in a house fire that killed all of his family but one sister. He was betrothed at the time of the fire. The woman he loved left him while he was still recovering in the hospital after taking one look at his burn injuries. Gabriel is sensitive about his burn scars, the worst of which he keeps hidden. Gabriel no longer believes in love, and he never expects to find a woman he not only likes but respects and in an unexpected way. Lucy never expected kindness and concern from Gabriel Fisher. The pregnant widow and the wounded hero…two people who have been hurt by those who should have stood by them. Sometimes all it takes is a little kindness, a little patience and someone to stick by you no matter what to understand true love.

I wish you happiness and good health.

Blessings and light,
Rebecca Kertz

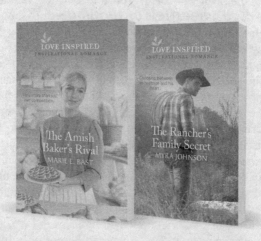

COMING NEXT MONTH FROM
Love Inspired

AN AMISH MOTHER FOR HIS TWINS
North Country Amish • by Patricia Davids

Amish widow Maisie Schrock is determined to help raise her late sister's newborn twins, but first she must convince her brother-in-law that she's the best person for the job. Nathan Weaver was devastated when his wife deserted him, but can he trust her identical sister with his children...and his heart?

THEIR SURPRISE AMISH MARRIAGE
by Jocelyn McClay

The last thing Rachel Mast expected was to end up pregnant and married—to her longtime beau's brother. But with her ex abruptly gone from the Amish community, can Rachel and Benjamin Raber build their marriage of convenience into a forever love?

THE MARINE'S MISSION
Rocky Mountain Family • by Deb Kastner

While ex-marine Aaron Jamison always follows orders, an assignment to receive a service dog and evaluate the company isn't his favorite mission—especially when trainer Ruby Winslow insists on giving him a poodle. But training with Ruby and the pup might be just what he needs to get his life back on track...

HER HIDDEN LEGACY
Double R Legacy • by Danica Favorite

To save her magazine, RaeLynn McCoy must write a story about Double R Ranch—and face the estranged family she's never met. But when ranch foreman Hunter Hawkins asks for help caring for the nieces and nephew temporarily in his custody, her plan to do her job and leave without forming attachments becomes impossible...

THE FATHER HE DESERVES
by Lisa Jordan

Returning home, Evan Holland's ready to make amends and heal. But when he discovers Natalie Bishop—the person he hurt most by leaving—has kept a secret all these years, he's not the only one who needs forgiveness. Can he and Natalie reunite to form a family for the son he never knew existed?

A DREAM OF FAMILY
by Jill Weatherholt

All Molly Morgan ever wanted was a family, but after getting left at the altar, she never thought it would happen—until she's selected to adopt little Grace. With her business failing, her dream could still fall through...unless businessman Derek McKinney can help turn her bookstore around in time to give Grace a home.

LOOK FOR THESE AND OTHER LOVE INSPIRED BOOKS WHEREVER BOOKS ARE SOLD, INCLUDING MOST BOOKSTORES, SUPERMARKETS, DISCOUNT STORES AND DRUGSTORES.

LICNM0621

Get 4 FREE REWARDS!

We'll send you 2 FREE Books plus 2 FREE Mystery Gifts.

Love Inspired books feature uplifting stories where faith helps guide you through life's challenges and discover the promise of a new beginning.

FREE Value Over $20

YES! Please send me 2 FREE Love Inspired Romance novels and my 2 FREE mystery gifts (gifts are worth about $10 retail). After receiving them, if I don't wish to receive any more books, I can return the shipping statement marked "cancel." If I don't cancel, I will receive 6 brand-new novels every month and be billed just $5.24 each for the regular-print edition or $5.99 each for the larger-print edition in the U.S., or $5.74 each for the regular-print edition or $6.24 each for the larger-print edition in Canada. That's a savings of at least 13% off the cover price. It's quite a bargain! Shipping and handling is just 50¢ per book in the U.S. and $1.25 per book in Canada.* I understand that accepting the 2 free books and gifts places me under no obligation to buy anything. I can always return a shipment and cancel at any time. The free books and gifts are mine to keep no matter what I decide.

Choose one: ☐ **Love Inspired Romance Regular-Print**
(105/305 IDN GNWC)

☐ **Love Inspired Romance Larger-Print**
(122/322 IDN GNWC)

Name (please print)

Address   Apt. #

City   State/Province   Zip/Postal Code

Email: Please check this box ☐ if you would like to receive newsletters and promotional emails from Harlequin Enterprises ULC and its affiliates. You can unsubscribe anytime.

> Mail to the **Harlequin Reader Service:**
> **IN U.S.A.:** P.O. Box 1341, Buffalo, NY 14240-8531
> **IN CANADA:** P.O. Box 603, Fort Erie, Ontario L2A 5X3

Want to try 2 free books from another series! Call 1-800-873-8635 or visit www.ReaderService.com.

*What happens when a tough marine and a sweet dog
trainer don't see eye to eye?*

Read on for a sneak preview of
The Marine's Mission *by Deb Kastner.*

"Oscar will be perfect for your needs," Ruby assured Aaron,
reaching down to scratch the poodle's head.

"That froufrou dog? No way, ma'am. Not gonna happen."

"Excuse me?" She'd expected him to hesitate but not
downright reject her idea.

"Look, Ruby, if you like Oscar so much, then keep him
for yourself. I need a man's dog by my side, not some…
some…"

"Poodle?" Ruby suggested, her eyebrows disappearing
beneath her long ginger bangs.

"Right. Lead me to where you keep the German
shepherds, and I'll pick one out myself."

"Hmm," Ruby said, rubbing her chin as if considering his
request, although she really wasn't. "No."

"No?"

"No," she repeated firmly. "First off, we don't currently
have a German shepherd as part of our program."

"I'd even take a pit bull." He was beginning to sound
desperate.

"Look, Aaron. Either you're going to have to learn to
trust me or you may as well just leave now before we start.
This isn't going to work unless you're ready to listen to me
and do whatever I tell you to do."

His eyebrows furrowed. "I understand chain of command, ma'am. There were many times as a marine when I didn't exactly agree with my superiors, but I understood why it was important to follow orders."

"Okay. Let's go with that."

"For me," Aaron continued, "following orders is black-and-white. My marines' lives under my command often depended on it. But as you can see, I'm having difficulty making that transition in this situation. We're not talking people's lives here."

"I disagree. We're very much talking lives—*yours*. You may not yet have a clear vision of what you'll be able to do with Oscar, but a service dog can make all the difference."

"Yes, but you just insisted the best dog for me is a *poodle*. I'm sorry, but if you knew anything about me at all, you'd know the last dog in the world I'd choose would be a poodle."

"And yet I still believe I'm right," said Ruby with a wry smile. Somehow, she had to convince this man she knew what she was doing. "I carefully studied your file before you arrived, Aaron, and specially selected Oscar for you to work with. I'm the expert here. So how are we going to get over this hurdle?"

"I have orders to make this work. How will it look if I give up before I even start the process?" He shook his head. "No. Don't answer that. It will look as if I wasn't able to complete my mission. That's never going to happen. I'll *always* pull through, no matter what."

Don't miss
The Marine's Mission *by Deb Kastner,*
available July 2021 wherever
Love Inspired books and ebooks are sold.

LoveInspired.com

IF YOU ENJOYED THIS BOOK, DON'T MISS NEW EXTENDED-LENGTH NOVELS FROM LOVE INSPIRED!

In addition to the Love Inspired books you know and love, we're excited to introduce even more uplifting stories in a longer format, with more inspiring fresh starts and page-turning thrills!

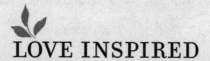

LOVE INSPIRED

Stories to uplift and inspire.

Fall in love with stories of faith, forgiveness and hope. Be inspired by characters overcoming life's challenges, and the promise of new beginnings.

LOOK FOR THESE LOVE INSPIRED TITLES ONLINE AND IN THE BOOK DEPARTMENT OF YOUR FAVORITE RETAILER!

LITRADE0621